# Whatever After
## COLD AS ICE

# Read all the Whatever After books!

# Whatever After

## COLD AS ICE

## SARAH MLYNOWSKI

Scholastic Inc.

for stella green
princess of locust valley

ISBN 978-0-545-62736-8

10 9 8 7 6 5 4 3 2 1          15 16 17 18 19

Printed in the U.S.A.   40
First printing 2015

# * chapter one *

## The Friendship Necklace

It's recess and I'm hanging upside down from the monkey bars. I should be concentrating on not falling. But instead I'm thinking about what I'm going to do with Robin and Frankie, my two best friends, when they come over after school. My plan is to make up dance routines and cook English muffin pineapple pizzas. But wouldn't it be so much more fun if I could take them through my magic mirror?

Yes! It would!

Don't get me wrong. Making up dance routines is a blast. And my English muffin pineapple pizzas are amazing. But as an after-school activity, you can't beat going through a magic mirror, can you?

No! You can't!

And yes. I have a magic mirror in my basement.

You don't believe me? It's the truth. The whole truth, and nothing but the truth. When my little brother, Jonah, and I moved from Naperville to Smithville, we discovered that when we knock on our basement mirror three times, it takes us into a fairy tale. Well, first the mirror starts to hiss, then it casts a purple light over the room, then it starts to swirl, and *then* it sucks us into a fairy tale.

So far, we've been to the stories of *Snow White*, *Cinderella*, *The Little Mermaid*, *Sleeping Beauty*, and *Rapunzel*. Robin even came with us once. But it doesn't count because she doesn't remember any of it. She was under a sleeping spell.

"Abby?" Frankie says, startling me out of my thoughts. "Abby, are you okay? You've been hanging there for a while. Your brain hasn't frozen, has it? It's so cold out!"

I laugh and grab the bars with both hands. "This isn't cold! It's forty-five degrees out. You don't even need gloves to do monkey bars in this town."

Smithville has the mildest winter ever. It doesn't even snow here. Not like it did in Naperville.

I don't miss the cold, but do I miss the snow.

"Well, my glasses are freezing onto my face," Frankie says.

Frankie's glasses' frames are bright red. I helped her pick them out. They look great against her straight dark hair and dark olive skin.

"We're going to stay inside at your house today, right?" she asks me, leaning against the bars. "No playing in the backyard?"

I jump down. "Indoors only," I tell her, smoothing back my own wavy brown hair. I feel a pang of excitement. I love when I get to host my best friends at my house, although the three of us can have fun anywhere.

Some people say bad things happen in threes, but I say *great* things happen in threes. Like best friends. FRA. That's what we call ourselves, FRA. It stands for Frankie, Robin, and me — Abby. We debated calling ourselves FAR or RAF, or even ARF, but I thought ARF sounded too much like a dog's bark. We decided FRA sounds like *f*riendship. FRA forever!

A few Wednesdays ago, we even made beaded friendship necklaces that spell out FRA.

We always get together on Wednesdays, because it's the only day none of us have after-school activities.

I glance across the school yard to see what Robin is doing. She's playing four square with Penny.

My stomach twists.

Robin's been spending a lot of time with Penny lately. Four square at recess. Sitting next to each other at lunch. Whispering to each other during class.

And Penny's not always so nice. I've seen her roll her eyes at me a few times. Twice she's called me bossy. Can you believe it? Bossy? Me?

Okay, fine, I can be a little bit bossy (especially with Jonah), but only because I have really good ideas. Like red glasses and making English muffin pineapple pizzas. Even Robin loves the pizzas. Last time we made them, she used the pineapple chunks to make eyes, a nose, and a mouth. It was adorable.

Here's the thing: I don't really like Penny. And Penny doesn't really like me. And I don't think Robin should spend any time with her at all.

I take a deep breath, trying to stay positive. I turn to face Frankie, who is now swinging on the monkey bars. This afternoon, FRA will have the best time ever.

Even though things feel a little funny between us and Robin.

Even though I can't take Frankie and Robin through the magic mirror.

There are a bunch of reasons why I can't take them. But the most important one is that I'm not supposed to tell anyone that the mirror exists. A fairy Jonah and I met in the story of *Snow White* warned us not to.

The recess bell rings, and Frankie and I hurry to line up.

Five hours left until FRA time. I can't wait.

At the end of the day, while Frankie is using the bathroom, I'm searching the hallway for Robin. I spot her at the water fountain.

"Ready for English muffin pineapple pizzas?" I ask her, shouldering my backpack.

Robin stands up and swallows hard. "Oh. Hey, Abby. Actually. I can't come over today. I have other plans."

"What plans?" I ask, my voice tight. "Do you have a doctor's appointment?"

"No," she says, fiddling with her beaded necklace. "I'm going to Penny's."

My stomach sinks to the bottom of my shoes. Penny? She's ditching us to spend more time with Penny?

"No. No, no, no."

"Excuse me?" Robin asks.

"No!" I say. "You can't ditch us to hang out with Penny! It's FRA day! Last week we went to your house, the week before we went to Frankie's, and today you're supposed to come to mine. That's the way we do it. For months. We have an order. A routine."

Robin looks down at her glittery sneakers. "Penny invited me to come over after school, and I want to go."

"Can't you go another day?" I ask, exasperated.

"No," she says. "I can't. Penny is busy on Tuesdays and Thursdays. The only day we both have free is Wednesdays."

"But the only day *we* have free is Wednesdays!" I shout. Then I try to catch my breath. Hmm. I don't really want Penny coming over, but I'd rather invite her along than lose Robin. "I guess

Penny can come to my house, too," I say. "It's fine. I probably have extra English muffins."

"That's okay," Robin says. "Maybe another time."

My eyes prick with tears. What is going on here? "Are you mad at us or something?"

"No," Robin answers, and our eyes lock. "I'm allowed to have other plans, aren't I? I can't just spend all my time with two people!"

"Why not?" I demand. "We're your best friends! You're supposed to spend all your time with your best friends!"

Robin tugs on one of her strawberry-blond curls and is quiet for a moment. "Penny is my best friend, too," she says.

*What?*

"No — no, she isn't," I stammer in shock. "Since when?"

"Since now," Robin says.

"*We're* your best friends. Me and Frankie. Not Penny. Penny isn't nice."

"I think she's fun," Robin says.

"Fun isn't the same as nice," I say. I cross my arms. "You can't be Penny's best friend and our best friend, too."

Robin pales. "Why not?"

"Because I said so," I respond, letting my voice rise. "You have to choose. It's either Penny. Or us."

Robin's eyes narrow. "If you're making me choose, then I choose Penny."

I gasp. I feel sad, but also really, really mad. My eyes narrow, too. "Then take off your necklace."

Robin's jaw drops. "My FRA necklace?"

"Yes!" I say, my voice cracking. "You're not our best friend anymore. You can't wear it. Go make necklaces with your new best friend, Penny. You can make Robin and Penny necklaces. *RP!*" I make the RP sound really loud, so it sounds extra ridiculous. Even more ridiculous than ARF did.

"You want me to take it off right now?" Robin asks quietly.

I nod. I'm afraid I'll start crying if I open my mouth.

"Fine." She pulls the leather strand over her head and throws it at me. "You keep it."

I stuff it in my backpack and run off to find Frankie.

My heart aches. FRA is over. From now on, it's just FA.

\*     \*     \*

8

At my house, I instruct Frankie to remove the R bead from *her* necklace.

"Do we really have to do that?" she asks, stretching out on my bedroom carpet.

"Yes," I say.

Her forehead wrinkles. "But why can't Robin have another best friend?"

"Because Penny is mean," I explain.

"But why does that matter to us? We don't have to be Penny's best friends, too."

"Frankie," I say patiently. "The whole point of having a best friend is that you choose that friend over everyone else. Robin chose Penny over us. She took off her necklace. Why should we have her initial on our necklaces? It doesn't make any sense."

"I guess so," Frankie says sadly.

I feel sad, too, but I don't want to give in to it. I pull my necklace off, untie it, and remove the R bead. Frankie does the same and I pick up the R bead from her hand.

"I won't throw them out," I say. "In case Robin comes to her

9

senses. I'm not a monster. If she apologizes, she can be back in our group."

Apologizes and promises to never talk to Penny again, that is.

I slip the beads and the necklace into my jewelry box and firmly shut the lid.

"I love your jewelry box," Frankie says, glancing over.

"Thanks," I say, biting my lip. I'm always a little nervous when my friends notice my jewelry box. My nana gave it to me. There are drawings of fairy tale characters on the box. But every time Jonah and I accidentally change the ending of a fairy tale, the drawing of the characters changes, too. I'm worried Frankie might notice that Sleeping Beauty is riding a bicycle, for instance, and I obviously can't explain why that's the case.

"Let's go make the pizzas!" I say, to get us out of my room.

We head down to the kitchen. I try very hard not to think about Robin as I slice open the English muffins, spoon out the tomato sauce, and sprinkle on the cheese.

"Now for the pineapple," I say. I carefully stand on a chair and open the cabinet door.

Peas. Corn. Peanut butter. No pineapple.

"How am I supposed to make English muffin pineapple pizzas without pineapple? Huh? Huh? It's impossible!" Tears prick the back of my eyes. I know I'm not really upset about the pineapple. The pineapple is not the real missing ingredient. The real missing ingredient is Robin.

She was our best friend. And even if she doesn't remember, she did go through the mirror with me once. We had a special bond.

Maybe I should tell Frankie about the magic mirror after all. Yes! I should. Then *we'll* have that special bond. We won't need Robin. We'll have each other.

"Frankie —" I start.

"Abby!" Jonah yells, rushing into the kitchen. "Look what I have!"

"What?" I ask, suddenly grateful that he interrupted me. What was I thinking? I'm not supposed to tell *anyone* about the mirror. The fairy from *Snow White* said it would be dangerous if I did.

"A Spider-Man watch!" Jonah cries. He juts out his small, seven-year-old arm. "Isaac got two for his birthday, and they didn't have the receipts to return them, so his parents said he could give one to me. Isn't it the best?"

"Yes, Jonah," I say. "The best." Sometimes I want to ruffle his brown hair, but I don't because I know that will embarrass him.

"I am going to wear it all the time," he says, admiring his wrist. "I'm never going to take it off."

"You'll probably want to take it off in the shower," Frankie says. "I once wore my watch in the shower, and it stopped working."

"Good point," Jonah says solemnly. "I will take it off to shower, but that's it."

I used to have a watch, too. But on our last trip through the mirror, I had to trade it for cab fare.

Now I have no watch.

No pineapple.

And no Robin.

I guess bad things do come in threes.

# * chapter two *

## Blame It on the Dog

"*aaabbbbby . . .*" a voice says that night.

I sit up in bed.

Did I just hear my name?

It's eleven forty-five and I haven't been able to fall asleep. I am too upset about the Robin situation. Also, my room is very cold. There may not be snow in Smithville, but our house — which is really old — is freezing. My parents keep trying to fix the heater but can't seem to get it right. Tonight I put on two pairs of socks, green flannel pajamas, a fleece sweatshirt, and a blue-and-white striped knit hat to go to bed. Yes. A hat.

Next I hear, *"Jonah . . ."*

The voice is faint and sounds a little bit like wind chimes. Is that Maryrose? Maryrose is the fairy that lives inside our magic mirror. At least, I think she lives inside it. Maybe she's trapped. Or maybe she's hiding. To be honest, we're not exactly sure what her housing situation is.

Anyway, is Maryrose really talking to me all the way from the basement? Did anyone else hear her?

*"Step through!"* I hear her say.

Step through the mirror? Does Maryrose want us to go into another fairy tale?

*"Please come!"* the voice chimes.

Part of me wants to yell, *Maryrose! We can't go through the magic mirror! I promised my parents that I wouldn't!* But I don't yell, because that would *so* wake my parents up.

Last time Jonah and I were visiting a fairy tale, my mom and dad woke up while we were away. They couldn't find us and called the police. Seriously. The police! Luckily, we came back through the mirror before the police actually arrived and before flyers with our pictures were taped all over the neighborhood with the word *MISSING* stamped across our foreheads. And luckily our parents didn't realize where we'd been.

But it was very, very close. My parents made us promise that we would never disappear at night again.

We promised.

So now we can't go.

Even though it's awesome. Even though I miss it, and Jonah misses it.

I cover my head with my pillow.

*Creak.*

Wait. Is that a door opening? Oh, no. Did Maryrose wake up my parents?

My parents will not be happy if they discover that there is a talking mirror in the basement. Although, if they did find out, then at least I wouldn't have to lie about it anymore.

But I bet they'd be pretty freaked out.

Maybe they would give the mirror away. Although it's bolted to the wall. If they couldn't get it off, maybe they would want to move. I'd have to go to another school. I bet Robin would miss me *then*.

I hear another creak.

The sound is coming from right next to my room. Which means it's my brother's door, and not my parents'. Maybe Maryrose woke up Jonah, too.

I glance at the clock. It's 11:56. Maryrose only lets us through the mirror at midnight.

Is Jonah sneaking down to the basement? Is he planning on going through the mirror without me? He better not be. He knows he's not allowed to do that.

"Jonah?" I say quietly.

No answer.

I push off my covers, jump out of bed, and hurry to stop him.

But he's not in the hallway.

Our puppy, Prince, is.

I should have guessed. Prince always sleeps in my brother's room. Right now, his ears are perked up like little triangles, meaning he's listening to something.

*"Come down!"* calls the voice in the basement.

Prince's tail wags. He's eyeing the staircase.

"Prince! No!" I whisper. I reach out to try and grab him, but he slips out of my hands and scurries down the stairs.

"Prince, stop!" I whisper furiously. "She's not talking to you! She's talking to *us*!"

It's not his fault he listened. The word *come* is one of his command words.

*He won't be able to go far*, I tell myself as I race down the stairs. I'm sure the basement door is closed. It always is. Prince may have pushed Jonah's door open, but that doesn't mean he'll be able to do the same to the basement door. On that one, you have to actually turn the handle. And anyway, even if he did get into the basement, it's not like the mirror would suck him inside. He'd have to knock three times on it for Maryrose to take him. And Prince might be smart, but he does not know how to knock.

I reach the basement door.

It's wide open.

Hmm.

Okay, I wasn't expecting that.

Who left the door open?

Probably Jonah. He's usually to blame when things go wrong, like most little brothers. Although maybe my parents *were* working in the basement before bed. All I know for sure is: It wasn't me. I am not to blame. I am never to blame. At least, not usually.

"Prince!" I call down. Should I go get him?

Yes. No. Yes.

No.

I can't. I specifically promised my parents I wouldn't go into the basement at night. If I take another step, then I am officially breaking my promise.

I do not like to break promises.

Unlike *Robin*.

"Prince! I'm waiting here for you," I whisper-yell.

Prince doesn't answer.

"Prince, if you come back upstairs, I'll give you a treat! Do you want some peanut butter? Mmmmm. Peanut butter. I'm eating peanut butter right now! It's delicious. I will eat all of it by myself if you don't come back up the stairs!"

*Come on, Prince, come on.* I do not want to stand here all night. It's cold! But at least I'm wearing two pairs of fuzzy socks, a fleece sweatshirt, and a hat.

I am making fake food-slurping sounds when I see it.

A purple light radiating up the stairs.

Oh no oh no oh no oh no.

I hear a whimper.

"Prince, no!" Without thinking, I run down the stairs.

Prince paws the glass. The reflection in the mirror starts to swirl like a tornado.

"Step back, Prince, step back!" I yell.

What do I do? Do I try and grab him? What if the mirror pulls me inside? I promised my parents I wouldn't go into the basement! And I can't go without Jonah!

My heart is racing. Do I go? Do I not go? Do I go? Do I not go?

The mirror turns into a vacuum cleaner, and with a loud slurp sound, Prince is sucked inside.

AHHHH!

I hold the banister tight so I don't get pulled along. After a few seconds, the mirror stops swirling.

"Abby?" I hear.

I turn around to see Jonah standing at the top of the stairs.

"What's happening?" he asks. "Where's Prince?"

I catch my breath, and then I say, "Prince escaped from your room and got into the basement and went through the mirror!" I try to keep my voice down so I won't wake my parents. But it's tough. This is a crisis.

Jonah's eyebrows shoot up. "Alone?"

"Of course alone. I'm here, aren't I?"

Jonah runs down the stairs. "ABBY! YOU LET MY DOG GO THROUGH THE MIRROR ALONE?"

"First of all, he's *our* dog," I huff. "And second of all, this isn't my fault. You didn't close your bedroom door properly. And you probably left the basement door open, too!"

"I did not," he says. "I wasn't even in the basement today. You were the one making up dance routines with Frankie down here."

Oops. He's not wrong. But I'm sure I closed it. I must have.

Jonah twists his bottom lip. "Do you think Prince will come back on his own?"

I stomp my foot. "No, of course I don't! How can he? He's just a dog!"

Jonah cocks his head to the side. "But he's a smart dog."

"But still a dog, Jonah. A *dog*. What do we do?"

He points to the mirror. "We go after him."

I feel frantic. "But we promised Mom and Dad we wouldn't!"

"But we don't have a choice." Jonah looks at his new Spider-Man watch. "We have to go now. It's midnight."

He's right. "Wait! Should we get shoes?"

"No shoes! No time! Let's go!" Jonah knocks once. The mirror makes a hissing sound. He knocks again and a purple haze falls over the room. He knocks one more time. Fast. The mirror swirls like a washing machine. I feel my curly brown hair twisting and twirling, and see Jonah's hair flapping like a flag in the wind.

"Maybe this time, it will be *Jack and the Beanstalk*," Jonah says hopefully. Jonah is always hoping it's *Jack and the Beanstalk*.

"That would be fun," I say. Then I add, "As long as the giant doesn't step on Prince."

Jonah pales.

"I'm only —"

Before I can say *joking*, the mirror sucks us both inside.

# ✳ chapter three ✳

## Brrrrr!

going through the mirror never hurts. It feels like you're walking through an open door.

This time, I land on something soft. And cold. It still doesn't hurt. It's just . . . cold.

Really cold.

Freezing, in fact.

I open my eyes and all I see is white. What is happening? Am I in a cloud? Are we in the story of *Aladdin*? Am I on a magic carpet?

I try to push myself up, but my hands sink lower.

I think I'm in snow.

I spit out what tastes like ice. Yes! It's snow. I roll over so I am finally looking up. There is blue sky everywhere. And I am definitely in a pile of snow. Snow! Beautiful, crisp white snow! How I've missed you!

Wait. What fairy tale takes place in the snow? Let's see. Well, *The Little Match Girl* takes place in the winter. . . .

WAIT.

Oh! My! Goodness!

Snow! So much snow!

We're in *Frozen*! We're in my favorite movie!

I've watched it about eight hundred times. I know all the songs by heart!

"I guess we're not in *Jack and the Beanstalk*," Jonah says, shaking white flakes out of his hair.

"Nope," I say with a laugh. "We're in —"

*"Frozen!"* I shout just as Jonah calls out, *"The Snow Queen!"*

"Huh?" Jonah asks. "Didn't you tell me *Frozen* was based on a fairy tale called *The Snow Queen*?"

My cheeks heat up despite the cold. He's right. Of course he's right. The movie *Frozen* is based on the story of *The Snow Queen*, which was written by Hans Christian Andersen. I can't believe I thought we were in the movie. Of course we're in *The Snow Queen*. Maryrose always takes us into the original stories.

"Yes! I knew that," I sputter. "I was just, um, testing you. We're in *The Snow Queen*. Obviously."

"Good," Jonah says. "I only know the *Frozen* version, but at least you know the original. So we know what's going to happen."

My nana is an English professor at a university in Chicago. Before we moved to Smithville, she used to read us the original fairy tales all the time. I paid a lot more attention than Jonah did. Also, ever since we started going through the mirror, I've been rereading a lot of the tales on my own. I've read *The Snow Queen*. A few times. Not as many times as some of the others.

It's broken up into seven stories, or chapters. It's really long.

And parts of it are kind of confusing.

"It's pretty here, huh?" Jonah asks.

"It definitely is," I agree. We're standing in the center of a flat, snowy field. It reminds me of a resort we went to last winter with our parents. They wanted us to try skiing.

Jonah loved it. I did not. I spent most of the time tripping over my skis as Jonah sailed down the mountain.

Anyway, the setting here looks a lot like that. Except without the chairlifts. Or skiers. Or people at all. It's just snow-covered mountains, pine trees, and blue sky as far as the eye can see. No houses or cabins in sight. I take a deep breath. The air is crisp, fresh, and cold, but the sun feels warm against my face.

Jonah examines his bare and now slightly red-with-cold hands. "Do you think our fingers will fall off?"

I bend my thumb back and forth. I wish I'd slept in mittens.

"Maybe," I say. Then I wiggle my toes inside my socks. Good thing I'm wearing two pairs. At least the snow is soft and powdery and not soaking into my feet. Not yet.

"I wish we'd put on shoes," I say. "Or better yet, *boots*."

"I'm wearing slippers," Jonah points out.

"Lucky," I say, looking down. His slippers are warm and fake-fur-lined. He got them for Hanukkah. I wish I had a pair.

Like me, Jonah also has on a fleece sweatshirt over his cozy charcoal-gray pj's. His sweatshirt has a hood. I reach up to adjust my striped knit hat. Suddenly, I'm glad our house in Smithville has heating problems.

Wait a sec . . .

Is it possible that Maryrose caused the recent heating problems? So that Jonah and I would sleep in really warm clothes and be better prepared to visit this story? Hmmm.

Jonah reaches out his ungloved hand and pulls me to my feet.

"We can't stay long," I warn, standing up and brushing ice chips off my flannel pajama bottoms. "Let's just get Prince and find our way back to the basement before Mom and Dad wake up. We have no idea what time it is at home."

"It's twelve-oh-one at home," Jonah says, holding up his wrist. "I'm wearing my Spider-Man watch."

"Oh! Right! Good. We'll wait and see how the time passes here." Sometimes a day in a fairy tale is an hour at home. Sometimes an hour in a fairy tale is an hour at home. The watches we wear from home keep track of the time back there.

Whenever we go through the mirror, we're always desperate to get back before seven A.M., when our parents come into our rooms to wake us up.

"It's pretty bright here now," Jonah says, blinking. "Maybe it's the middle of the day? Around noon?"

"Feels like that," I say. "We want to be out of here before it gets dark." Without the sun, we'd definitely turn into icicles.

"Look at all the snow!" Jonah cries out, scooping both arms full of it. "I miss snow!"

"Me too," I admit.

"It's like Naperville but even better! Let's build a snow fort!" he exclaims, crouching down.

"Jonah, I just told you we're in a rush. We have to find Prince, and we have to find the portal home." The portal home can be anything. A chimney. A window. A mirror. And we never know what it is until we knock on it. "No snow forts. At least, not until we find Prince and the portal home."

"What about a snowman?"

"Jonah, we are not making a snowman!"

"Hey! It's like I'm Anna and you're Elsa," he teases. "You're refusing to build a snowman with me!"

I smile. "You know we're not going to meet Elsa or Anna, right?"

His face falls. "What? How come?"

"They weren't in the original story."

He pouts. "What about Olaf? Kristoff?"

"No and no."

"Is there even a snow.queen?" he asks with a sigh.

"Of course there's a snow queen," I say, struggling to remember everything. "That's the name of the story. But she's much, much different from what you'd expect. She's evil and scary."

His eyes light up. "Really?" Jonah loves the evil and scary parts of stories.

I nod.

"Can you tell me the original story?" Jonah asks.

I rub my hands together to warm them. "Let's look for Prince while I tell you." Suddenly, I have a sinking feeling in my stomach. "Jonah, what if Prince isn't in this story?"

"Huh?"

"We didn't go through the mirror at the same time he did. He could be in a totally different fairy tale from ours. Like *Beauty and the Beast*! Or *The Princess and the Pea*!" I swallow hard. Prince could be taking a snooze on a hundred mattresses while we're trekking through mountains of snow to find him.

"No, he's here," Jonah says, his voice confident.

"And how do you know that?"

"Because those are his paw prints."

Jonah points up ahead in the snow. I see the small paw print —
a circle with four smaller circles on top of it. It looks like the
outline of a flower. There's not just one paw print, either. There's
a whole line of them leading through the field and toward one of
the mountains.

Yay!

"Prince *is* here!" I say, relieved. At least we are not on a fairy
tale wild-goose chase. "Let's go," I add, tugging Jonah's arm.
Then I stop when I realize another potential problem. "How do
we know for sure that those are Prince's paw prints and not, say,
a wolf's, or something?"

Jonah's eyes light up again. "Like the wolf from *Little Red
Riding Hood*? You think he's here, too?"

That's another one of Jonah's favorite stories. Jonah only
likes — and remembers — the ones where people get eaten or
lose toes.

"No, Jonah, I don't think the wolf from *Little Red Riding Hood*
is here. Have you noticed the piles of snow?"

"Yeah, but couldn't there be another fairy tale that takes
place in the winter? It's not always summer in Little Red Riding
Hood's forest, is it? It must snow there sometimes, too."

Oh. Right. "Good point," I sigh. Jonah's making *a lot* of good points. "So we might not even be in *The Snow Queen*?" I groan.

"Maybe not."

"I guess we'll find out soon enough." I motion for my brother to follow me. My foot sinks into the snow with every step. My socks are starting to get slightly wet. Great.

I hear Jonah's slippers crunch the snow beside me. "In case we are in *The Snow Queen*," he says, "why don't you just tell me the story like you were going to?"

"Fine," I say. "But it's really long. And kind of strange. I'll try and give you the short version. There are two kids, Kai and Gerda. They're neighbors and best friends, and Gerda's grandma takes care of them. But then one day, Kai disappears. Everyone says he died, but Gerda doesn't believe it. She thinks that the Snow Queen came and put Kai under her spell. And she's right! The Snow Queen numbed Kai all the way to his heart with her freezing powers! Gerda decides she's going to find him. So she goes on a search. She meets all these weird people along the way. At one point, a band of robbers grabs her!"

"A band?" Jonah interrupts. "Like a singing group?"

"No. A band, like a bunch of people."

"Then why is it called a band?"

."I don't know," I say. "It just is."

"Are you sure they don't sing?"

"Yes," I say, trudging over a mound of snow. "I'm sure. They're not that kind of band."

At the word *band*, Jonah poses like he's playing a guitar.

"I said they're *not* that kind of band."

"I know. But it's a fun pose."

I slip on a patch of ice and fall on my behind. Ouch. I push myself back up and straighten my hat. "Can I go on with the story now?"

Jonah makes one more strum on his imaginary guitar. "Yes. Go on."

As I talk, we continue following the paw prints through the snowy field.

"In the band of robbers, there's a little robber girl. And this girl lets Gerda escape. And she lends her a reindeer."

"Sven!"

"Not Sven. Just a reindeer." I step around another circle of ice.

"Still. I have always wanted to see a reindeer." Jonah tries to run up a steep snowbank as we talk.

"Careful, Jonah," I say. "Well, we might see a reindeer, depending on where we are in the story. If we're even in *The Snow Queen*. Anyway. The little robber girl helps Gerda escape. Gerda finally makes her way over to the Snow Queen's ice castle. She sees Kai. He is definitely under the Snow Queen's spell. She hugs him and cries, and her tears and then his tears melt the spell and unfreeze him. He snaps out of his trance and follows her home."

Jonah bends down to scoop up some snow and lets it fall from his hand. "What happens to the Snow Queen?"

I shrug. "Nothing. She's not there."

"What do you mean?"

"I don't know. She's away at the end of the story. Traveling or something."

"Convenient," Jonah says.

"Seriously," I agree. We've reached the foot of a mountain. The paw prints go up and behind one of the trees. We follow them. I hope he didn't climb too high.

"Well, the story wasn't *that* complicated. Or long."

"There's a bunch of other stuff that doesn't make sense," I explain. "Like, there's a troll."

"A troll? A nice troll?"

"No. He breaks a mirror, and the broken pieces fly into people's eyes and hearts and harden and freeze them."

Jonah furrows his eyebrows. "I thought the Snow Queen froze people's hearts."

"Yeah. That's the confusing part. I don't know. Just stay away from broken mirrors, 'kay?"

He nods. " 'Kay."

I feel something wet and cold land on my nose.

I look up. Snowflakes. A million of them, coming down hard. It's snowing.

"Pretty!" Jonah says. "It's like we're in a snow globe!"

They *are* kind of pretty. They look like confetti. "We should keep going," I say. Except, when I look down, I realize the problem with the pretty snowflakes. "Oh, no! The paw prints are being buried in the snow! I can't tell which way Prince went!"

"Shhh!"

"Don't shush me, Jonah, this is a real problem!" Now that we're walking up the mountain and between the trees, I can't feel the sunlight, and my cheeks are starting to freeze.

"Did you hear that?" Jonah whispers.

"Hear what?"

Then I hear it.

*Ruff!*

"Prince!" I holler as a bunch of snowflakes fall on my eyelashes. "Is that you? Prince, where are you?"

*Ruff, ruff, ruff!*

Prince! It's him!

*Ruff, ruff!*

I roll my eyes as I realize where the barks are coming from.

The top of the mountain.

Thanks, Prince. Thanks a lot.

# * chapter four *

## Moving On Up

L et's go, let's go!" Jonah urges as we try to hike up the snowy hill. The mountain is packed with evergreen trees. It feels like a maze. A snowy maze on a mountain. At least it stopped snowing.

"This would be a lot easier in a chairlift," I pant.

"You can do it!" he says. Jonah takes wall-climbing lessons on the weekends. I do not. You might think that climbing lessons wouldn't make a difference in this situation, since we are climbing a snowy mountain and not a wall, but it does.

I am not so good at it. Plus, my legs are half-numb.

"Step with your heel," he says.

"I am trying to, Jonah. But I'm wearing socks! And anyway, what does that even mean to *step with my heel*? What else would I be stepping with?"

"You should have worn boots," he says. "Or slippers."

I narrow my eyes. Then I bend down, pack a snowball in my very cold and slightly stiff fingers, and throw it at the back of his head.

*Bull's-eye!*

"Hey!" Jonah cries.

I can't help giggling. "Sorry! It was an accident! My limbs aren't working correctly in this cold."

"Oh yeah?" Jonah laughs. He brushes the snow off his shoulders and then runs ahead until I can't see him.

"Don't you dare, Jonah!" I yell.

He doesn't answer.

I crouch down and pack another snowball. My fingers are freezing, but it will be worth it when I win this snowball fight. "I'm ready for you!" I yell. I cautiously creep ahead.

Nothing.

Nothing.

Noth —

A huge snowball comes soaring toward me like a big white, scary football. I duck and fling the snowball in my hand.

Jonah's snowball lands on the ground beside me.

"Missed me, missed me!" I holler.

"Abby!" Jonah says. "You hit someone in the shoulder!"

"You, I hope!" I cackle.

He comes running toward me. "No. You hit a kid!"

"What?" I ask. "Who?"

I look around. We've made it to the top of the mountain, I see. And a kid is standing there, and he has a dusting of snow on his shoulder. He's about my age, with shaggy light brown hair and a pale face. He's wearing gray pants, boots (which make me very jealous), a navy sweater, and a green scarf. And gloves. Navy gloves. Wonderful, warm, navy gloves. I'm even more jealous of those than I am of his boots. It's all I can do not to rip them right off him. Instead, I force myself to not act like a lunatic and to apologize.

"Hi there," I say to him. "I'm so sorry I hit you with my snowball. That was meant for my brother!"

He doesn't answer me. Instead, he's picking branches off the ground.

Is he going to try and poke me with one?

"I really am sorry," I say.

Instead of answering, the boy picks up another branch and starts walking away.

"What's wrong with him?" Jonah asks me.

I grimace. "I hope I didn't hit him in the head and give him a concussion. Excuse me?" I say to the boy. "Are you okay?"

This time, the boy looks back toward us. But instead of looking *at* us, it's like he's looking *through* us.

"He has zombie eyes," Jonah whispers, his voice trembling with excitement.

The boy totally does have zombie eyes. The irises are green, but his pupils aren't black. They're white. It's very creepy.

"Flowers," the boy says, but then he continues walking away from us.

"Huh?" I ask. "Did he say *flowers*? There are no flowers in the middle of the winter."

"Not true," Jonah says. "There are hellebores."

"Huh?"

"Hellebores! It's a type of flower! And also phlox! We learned about them in school."

"I don't believe that."

"It's true!"

"If you say so, Jonah," I say, and look ahead to see the boy still walking. "Maybe he said *follow*, not *flower*. Maybe he meant we should follow him?"

Cautiously, we follow the boy around the trees. And then past the last tree and into a clearing. I close my eyes as the sunlight kisses my face and warms me instantly.

Ahhh. Much better.

"Wow," says Jonah. "Look at that."

I flick my eyes open.

Oh, wow.

Wow, wow, wow.

We *are* in the story *The Snow Queen*.

I know this because right in front of us is the ice castle.

It's not a castle exactly. It looks more like a really wide and tall igloo. The walls are built of tiny ice bricks that glitter like diamonds in the sunlight. The roof is flat, though, with a railing made of icicles.

"Whoa. This is the coolest place ever," Jonah says.

The mystery boy does not seem fazed by the igloo castle. He walks right through the snowy yard and through the ice-coated doors.

"Why did he go inside with a bunch of sticks?" I wonder aloud.

"Maybe he's building a fire," Jonah says. "It must be cold in there. No. Wait! I bet they're arms!"

"Huh?"

"Snowmen arms! Look up on the roof!"

I look up on the roof. Standing on it are two fully built snowmen with hats, carrots for noses, coal for eyes, and branches for arms. There's another in-process snowman that has a nose and a hat but no arms.

"And look there," Jonah adds, pointing over to the side of the yard. There are three other snowmen, a small snow fort, and impressions in the yard that look like snow angels. "This kid must spend a lot of time playing in the snow."

I gasp. "Jonah! I know who that kid is. It must be Kai!"

"Who?"

"The boy! From the story. Gerda's friend! The one the Snow

Queen put under her spell. Didn't he seem like he was under a spell?"

"Definitely," Jonah says. "A zombie spell. A snowman-making zombie spell."

Then we hear it again.

*Ruff! Ruff! Ruff! Ruff!*

My heart jumps. Prince's bark! It sounds much closer now.

"Where's that coming from?" I ask.

*Ruff!*

I look up once more.

It's Prince! He's on the roof! He charges toward the railing, knocking over one of the snowmen as he goes.

I've never been happier to see his little furry brown body. And he sees us! He's barking at us!

"Hi, Prince, hi!" I call out, hopping on my tiptoes so I can see him better.

"Can you jump down?" Jonah calls up to him.

"I think it's too far," I say. It's about two stories up. "Don't jump down!" I yell. "We'll come and get you, Prince. We love you!"

*Ruff, ruff!*

Suddenly, a woman — well, more like a teenager — rises onto the roof beside Prince. Her hair is silver, long, and curly, her eyes are ice blue, and she's wearing a long white dress and a white fur cloak. Her skin sparkles like it's covered in body glitter.

My breath catches in my throat.

She's the Snow Queen. She has to be. I can't take my eyes off her. Even though she's the queen of cold, she's as mesmerizing as fire.

"Stop making such a racket, you mutt," she says to Prince, her voice as cold as ice.

Her words send a pulse of fear through my entire body. Jonah slinks behind me.

"Is that Elsa?" Jonah asks.

"That is *not* Elsa," I say softly. This snow queen is terrifying. "Where did she come from?" I wonder out loud. "Did she just magically appear?" Kai pops up onto the roof next, holding the sticks in his hand. He inserts them into the snowman that was missing arms. "Did he just appear, too?" I ask.

"No, they both came up a staircase in the middle of the roof. It's behind Prince."

Aha.

*Ruff, ruff, ruff, ruff!* Prince calls to us. He's jumping up and down. Exactly like he does when we get home from school. His whole body is trembling with excitement.

"Stop that yapping immediately," the Snow Queen tells him, "or you'll regret it."

"Oh, no," I murmur. It feels like the moment before a storm. The air gets heavy and dark. Something awful is about to happen, I know it.

Jonah is trying to motion with his hands for Prince to be quiet, but instead of listening, our puppy just wags his tail harder and barks even louder.

The Snow Queen steps closer to Prince. "Don't say I didn't warn you," she says. Then she leans toward him and puckers her lips. What is she doing?

"Prince!" I yell. "Run, Prince, run!"

With her lips all rounded, the Snow Queen looks like she's blowing Prince a kiss. But it's not a kiss. I can actually see the air that comes out of her mouth. It's like steam from a kettle. A tiny white tornado.

Prince lifts his paws and starts to run.

The kiss hits him, and he slows down, looking dazed. The

Snow Queen puckers up again and another tornado shoots out of her mouth.

"I'm scared," Jonah says, his voice trembling.

"Prince!" I yell again.

A sad sound escapes Prince's doggie mouth and then he freezes in mid-motion. He solidifies in place. One paw up about to take a step, his tail still on high alert. His fur gets a white glaze all over. He looks like a dog who's been locked in a freezer for too long. He looks like he has freezer burn. He looks —

I gasp. I feel a stab in my heart.

He looks frozen.

The Snow Queen just froze my dog.

# * chapter five *

## Dogsicle

n o!" Jonah and I both scream. "No, no, no!"

I'm too shocked to move.

But Jonah starts running toward the igloo castle. Then he slips and falls.

My heart pounds as I try to help him up.

"She hurt our dog!" Jonah calls out. "She turned him into a Popsicle! No, a *dogsicle*!"

"Is he —" I can't say it. He can't be dead. He just *can't* be. I feel a lump in my throat.

"His eyes are blinking. Look! He's still alive. He's just frozen! You froze our dog, you evil person, you!" Jonah waves his fist at the roof.

"Shhh! Jonah!" I hiss, squeezing his arm.

The Snow Queen takes a step toward the railing. "Come here, children. Come closer. Come play with Kai. Have you ever made a snow angel?"

Kai looks like he's in a trance. He's now lying on his back on the roof, flapping his arms, making, I'm guessing, a snow angel.

"She's creepy," Jonah whispers. "Do we have to go to her?"

"I don't know," I whisper back. "We need to save Prince, but I don't want the Snow Queen to put us under her spell. Then we're all in trouble."

"Which spell? The zombie spell or the dogsicle one?"

"Either!"

"Come on, children," the Snow Queen says. "Come closer." She puckers up her lips. *"MM-WAH!"* The white tornado steam shoots from her lips. It's heading right toward us.

I take Jonah's hand and yank him back, away from the yard. "Run! She's blowing us a magical kiss!"

Jonah pulls his hand away. "We can't leave Prince!"

"We have to," I say, feeling awful but knowing we don't have a choice. "We'll come back and get him when the Snow Queen isn't here! In the original story, she's always traveling! We'll come back when she's out of town."

"But how will we know when she's out of town?" Jonah demands.

More tornado steam is headed our way.

"I don't know. But we've got to get out of here NOW. We have to run back down the mountain!" I yank Jonah's arm, and we take off.

"Follow me!" Jonah shouts. "There's a section with no trees! We'll slide down. It's a straight shot to the bottom! It'll be faster."

I follow him, my breath catching as I run. "Slide?" I ask, worried. "Like on a sled?"

"Yes!" he calls back, still running. "Except without the sled."

"On what, then?"

"On our stomachs!"

"No, no, no! We'll break our noses!"

We reach the clearing and hesitate at the edge. It looks steep. Very steep.

"Can we roll?" Jonah asks.

"I think it's safer to go on our backs. Like a waterslide."

Jonah nods, a gleam in his eye. "See you at the bottom! Race ya!" He takes three steps back and then runs and does a flying leap down the hill.

"Oh, boy." I hope I don't regret this. I quickly launch myself feetfirst.

I go fast.

The ice is hard against my back, and the momentum keeps pushing my head down, even though I want to sit up and see where I'm going. The wind, ice, and snow bite at my cheeks. I have to close my eyes because they start to burn from ice pellets. I wish I had goggles. I wish I had a helmet. I wish I had a toboggan.

"Don't hit a tree. Don't hit a tree," I repeat to myself over and over like a mantra.

But I admit it. If I weren't afraid of slamming into a tree, this would be kind of fun.

Jonah certainly thinks so. I can hear him yelling, "Wahoo!" far ahead of me.

"You're almost there!" he calls out.

I wrench my eyes open.

This side of the mountain leads to a frozen lake at the bottom. A frozen lake I'm about to crash into.

I brace myself for impact.

"Yowza!" I scream as I slide, slide, slide across the lake, spinning like a top. When I eventually stop spinning, I try to sit up but feel dizzy.

I can't see the Snow Queen or her scary breath anymore. Does that mean we lost her? I just hope we haven't lost Prince, too. I try not to think about how we're going to get back up that mountain.

Now where's Jonah?

I spot him a few hundred feet away on the other side of the lake.

"That was amazing," he says as he glides toward me.

"If you say so," I reply.

All right, I'll admit it. It was kind of amazing.

"So what do we do now?" he asks me, looking worried.

Good question. I look toward the mountain. "We have to get back up there to unfreeze Prince. But we have to wait until the Snow Queen leaves."

"But how will we know when she leaves?" my brother persists.

"Let me think." I push myself up off the ice. In all the body-sledding excitement, I forgot about the cold, but now that I'm standing still, I feel the chill all over my body. I rub my hands against my fleece sweatshirt. I wish I was wearing two fleece sweatshirts. Or maybe a fleece snowsuit.

"Maybe we wait a few hours and then climb back up?" Jonah suggests.

"I guess so," I say. "Although a heated helicopter would be nice."

His eyes widen. "I would be an amazing helicopter pilot."

I snort. "I'm sure you would, Jonah. But seriously, I don't know how long we can stay out here dressed the way we are. If the sun goes down, we're going to be in trouble. We'll freeze."

Jonah glances at his watch. "My watch says it's one. How many hours do you think have passed since we got here?"

The sun is lower now. "It feels like around three, right?"

He nods. "So an hour at home is about three hours here?"

"Seems right," I say. I try to calm my nerves. We've been gone for only an hour. My parents are still asleep. We'll get home before they wake up. They won't find out we broke our promise.

I hesitate. "Hey, Jonah? Maybe I should wear the watch. For safekeeping."

He clutches his wrist protectively. "No way! It's my Spider-Man watch, and I want to wear it! I'll keep it safe. I swear."

"As safe as you kept Dad's iPhone? Or Mom's laptop? Or your Karate Crocs game?"

In the last month, Jonah left Dad's iPhone on the *corner* of a counter, where it fell off and shattered. Then he somehow and for some unknown reason removed the G and K keys from Mom's keyboard. And he dropped his Karate Crocs game in the toilet.

He is not good with electronics.

"I'll be careful," he says. "Hey! Wanna go skating while we wait for the Snow Queen to leave?"

"Did you sneak skates through the mirror, too?"

"No. I wish. I meant pretend skating. Like this." He attempts to skate across the ice in his slippers. "Or we should play hockey!" He pretends to run as if he's chasing a puck. He ends up tripping and landing elbows-down on the ice.

That's when I hear it.

A loud crack.

Oh, no. I do not like the sound of cracks. Cracks do not mean good things. Not for bones. Or for mirrors. Or for frozen lakes.

"Jonah? What was that?"

Jonah is staying perfectly still.

The ice is splintering around him.

"Abby," he says slowly. "I think we have a problem."

"No kidding," I reply.

"What do I do?" he squeaks.

I try not to panic. "Don't move! I don't want you to make it worse."

"But if I don't move, how do I get off the lake that's about to break?"

Good point. "Okay, maybe move. But can you move really, really slowly toward me?"

He stands up carefully. The ice holds.

"Now step toward me," I say.

He takes one step. So far, so good.

I hold my breath.

He takes another step. Another.

*Crack! Crack! Crack!* It sounds like popcorn popping. A spider-web of cracks spreads across the ice.

The cracks reach all the way to me.

Jonah and I lock eyes. Then . . . *crack!* The lake breaks, and both of us plunge into the frigid water.

# ✳ chapter six ✳

## The Worst Pool Ever

**t**he cold water feels like thousands of needles piercing my body.

I kick and splash to stay afloat. Ouch, ouch, ouch! The water is so cold! I have never felt water so cold!

*Where is Jonah? Is he okay?*

I strain to lift my head above the water. My hat has fallen off and probably sunk to the bottom.

I'm surrounded by huge chunks of ice floating in the water. Great. Just great. I don't like swimming in regular water. Never mind freezing-cold water filled with ice shards poking me and trying to turn me into a human ice cube. At least there are no sharks in lakes.

There are no sharks in lakes, right?

RIGHT?

"Jonah!" I scream. "Jonah, are you okay?"

I don't hear him. I don't see him! I have to save Jonah! Where is he?

"I'm here!" he yells back. His left arm is in the air, and he's paddling toward me. "I'm okay! Kind of! It's hard to tread water when I'm trying to keep the watch dry! But don't worry, Abby! I won't let anything happen to the watch! I promise! I will keep it safe no matter what!"

"Don't worry about the watch!" I yell back. "Just worry about not drowning!"

My toes and fingers are starting to freeze. *Must keep swimming! Must not drown!* I need a plan.

Yes. A plan!

What is my plan? How am I going to not drown?

Oh! I know. I need to get out of the water. I need to get to land.

But where is the land?

I try to grab on to a chunk of ice that looks secure, but it breaks off in my hand. What do I do? I need to think. Can't think. Brain is too cold. Teeth ch-ch-ch-chattering. Feet too cold. Can't move.

Slam.

*Ouch!*

Something heavy just hit me in the face. A shark is attacking my face!

No. We're in a lake. There are no sharks in lakes. RIGHT?

I hear, "Grab the rope!"

Rope?

I take another look at the floating heavy thing beside me. Oh! It is a rope! I take hold of it with my icy hands.

"Hold on tight," I hear.

I do my best to squeeze my hands around the rope and hold on. I force every part of me to wrap my legs around the end. I feel it being yanked. I am being pulled toward the shore. I keep scraping against shards and chunks of ice. "Jo-nah, too!" I shout. "Jonah, too!" At least, I think I shout it. I can't tell if my mouth is actually moving.

Finally, I feel hard ice under my feet. Land. Ice land. But still land.

"Put this on," a voice says. A large brown blanket covers my soaking-wet shoulders. Ahh. Warmth. S-s-s-o good.

"Thank-k-k you," I say, my teeth chattering. "J-J-Jonah. My brother. We have to get him. Give me the r-r-rope. I have to go b-b-back in."

"We got him," an evergreen tree says.

The tree saved him! Hurrah!

No. Wait. That's my frozen brain talking. Or maybe my eyeballs have iced over. I blink multiple times. Standing beside me is a small, talking evergreen tree. It has a brown trunk and many green pine needles protruding from its body.

It also has blue eyes and a long pointy nose.

It takes me a few seconds to realize that the tree is actually a girl. She is wearing brown pants and a dark green coat that has pine needles taped to it. Her face is painted dark green and she's wearing a hat that also has pine needles on it. A tuft of blond hair peeks out from under the hat.

It's a girl in a tree costume!

Is it Halloween in this kingdom?

The girl looks young. About my age. There's a woman also dressed as a tree, standing behind her. She's wearing a patch over one of her eyes and is glaring at me with her other one.

The girl points to the other side of the lake and motions to a shivering lump sitting in the snow. I realize that it's not actually a lump — it's my brother wrapped in a brown blanket. Two other trees are standing beside him. Make that two people in tree costumes.

"Thank-k-k you!" I manage to say. "My brother is okay?"

"Yup." The tree girl smiles. "It's your lucky day."

"Can I ask why you're dressed like trees?" I ask, still shaking. "Is that the style here?"

"It's *our* style," the girl says and laughs.

Hmm. What does she mean?

"Why were you guys on the lake, anyway?" she asks me.

"It's a long story," I say. "But basically, the Snow Queen stole our dog."

Her blue eyes widen. "The Snow Queen? Really? Her castle is around here?"

"Right up the mountain," I say.

"No way," the tree girl squeals. "I wish I could meet her." She turns to the tree woman with the eye patch. "Mother! The Snow Queen lives close by!"

The tree woman glares at the tree girl and me with her good eye. "Get in the sled."

*Kind of rude*, I think.

The tree girl touches my wet arm. "Hey, you better change into something dry before you get sick. Do you want to borrow some clothes?"

"Thank you SO much," I say, feeling very grateful. "Do you happen to have extra shoes, too? Or boots? I can barely feel my toes."

"I'm sure we have something in the sled," she says. "Follow me."

"Can Jonah come, too?" I ask. "He's probably freezing."

She laughs again. "Oh, yeah, you're both coming."

A weird reply, but I wave Jonah over. He's standing up now, bundled in the blanket. I see that he lost his slippers in the lake. How many pairs of slippers have we lost in fairy tales by now? A million?

"Mother doesn't want to get too close to the Snow Queen," the tree girl whispers. "But I would love to meet her. She has freezing powers! I wish I had freezing powers."

"She doesn't seem very nice, though," I say. "She uses her powers to hurt people."

Tree Girl shrugs. "Whatever."

Jonah reaches us. His teeth are chattering.

"You okay?" I ask, putting my arm around him.

"Of course! That-t-t was fun."

I resist the urge to roll my eyes. Only Jonah would find almost drowning in an ice lake fun.

"She's giving us clothes," I say as we follow Tree Girl deeper into the forest. The three other tree women are not far behind us. "Isn't that nice of her?"

"Thank-k-k you," Jonah says to Tree Girl. Then he whispers to me, "Why are they all d-d-dressed up as t-t-trees? Are we going to have to dress as t-t-trees?"

"I don't know," I say. "But I'd rather dress as a tree than stay in my sopping-wet sweatshirt and pajamas."

"Me t-t-too," he says.

"It's right there," Tree Girl says, pointing.

It takes me a while to see the sled because it's white and blends in with the snow. But then I make it out, and I realize that there's a white-and-gray horse standing in front of it.

Wait. It's not a horse. It's bigger. And it has two huge, long gray antlers coming from its head.

"Is that a reindeer?" I ask.

"Yes," Tree Girl says.

"Cool!" Jonah exclaims. "I've always wanted to see a reindeer."

"The proper name is actually 'caribou,'" I say. This caribou has a small bell around its neck.

"Well, I prefer 'reindeer,'" the reindeer says.

I blink in surprise. Did the reindeer just speak? No. I must have imagined it. I stare at the creature.

"Reindeer got your tongue?" the reindeer says.

My brain must have cold-lake damage. "Did anyone else hear the reindeer talk?" I ask.

"I did!" Jonah exclaims. "You can talk?" he asks the reindeer.

"Yeah," the reindeer scoffs. He has a very deep voice. "So can you. Should we both get medals?"

I laugh from shock. I can't help it. A reindeer is making fun of us. Of all the things I thought could happen when I went through the mirror in my basement tonight, this was not one of them.

Although now that I think about it, maybe the reindeer in the original Snow Queen story did talk?

"Put these on," Tree Girl orders, reaching into the back of a sled and passing me a lump of clothes. There is a ton of stuff in the sled. Some silver forks and spoons and plates, some picture frames, more blankets, more clothes. Is that a statue? And a painting? Weird.

I shake out the outfit. It's furry. And white. "Is this a polar bear costume?" I ask.

"Yes," Tree Girl says.

"Mine's a penguin costume," Jonah says. "I've always wanted a penguin costume! And it has a hood!"

I cover myself with the blanket so I can have some privacy from all the tree women. Then I peel off my wet sweatshirt, pajamas, and socks. I step into the white furry one-piece. There's a side zipper. Then I pull on the white furry mittens and white furry booties. The costume head is separate. It's also white and furry but has a black nose, holes for my mouth and eyes, and two furry white ears. I put it on. Not because I want to look like a polar bear but because my face is really cold and my wet hair has turned into icicles.

I drop the blanket and reemerge.

I see Jonah. Jonah sees me. We both laugh hysterically.

"Is that you, Abby?" he asks.

"It is," I say.

Jonah's costume is even more ridiculous than mine. His arms and legs are black, but there is a giant white oval over his stomach, and his booties are bright yellow. At least his costume doesn't cover his face. There's just a yellow beak and white eyes on the hood.

"Is it a costume holiday in this kingdom?" I ask Tree Girl.

"Sure," she says, with another laugh. "A costume holiday."

I have a bad feeling I can't put my finger on.

"What's this kingdom called?" I wonder out loud.

"It's not a kingdom," she says. "It's a republic. There's no queen or king."

"But what about the Snow Queen? Isn't she *the* queen?" I ask.

"She has freezing powers, but she doesn't run the republic. No one runs the Republic of Blizzard."

"Then why is she called the queen?"

She shrugs. "Maybe Queen is her last name?"

Jonah licks his lips. "That's what the republic is called? Blizzard?"

"Yes," Tree Girl says.

"Like the ice cream at Dairy Queen? I love those. I would totally have a DQ Blizzard now."

"Seriously, Jonah?" I say. "Ice cream? Now?"

He shrugs. "I'm hungry." He taps Tree Girl on the shoulder. "Is there anything to eat in the sled?"

"We have hot chocolate," she says. She reaches back into the sled and pulls out a thermos and then pours the liquid into two mugs.

I take a big sip. *Yummm.* I am not exaggerating when I say this might be the most delicious thing I've ever tasted in my entire life. The warm liquid makes my body melt in the best possible way.

"Now, that hits the spot," I say. "Thank you," I tell the tree girl again. "For everything."

"It's nothing," she says, turning red and looking at the icy ground.

"No, really. You guys saved our lives. I wish I could get you a thank-you present! Like chocolates." I think of poor Kai. "Or flowers!"

"I'm allergic to flowers," she says. "They make me sneeze."

"Then definitely no flowers," I say. "But seriously, we'd freeze without these costumes. We'll give them back to you when we're done with them. I mean, I'm not exactly sure how we'll do that since we don't live nearby and we're not staying long. Oh! Maybe we could trade you the costumes for our pajamas? They'll dry eventually. They're very comfortable. And almost brand-new." We've probably left behind even more pajamas than slippers in various fairy tales.

"Yeah! I can wear this costume on Halloween!" Jonah squeals, patting his penguin belly.

The reindeer snorts. "You guys are clueless."

I'm so startled to hear him talking again that his words take a second to register. "Excuse me?"

The reindeer looks right at me and starts blinking. Again and again and again. What's he doing?

"Are you okay?" I ask him. "Is something in your eye?"

He sighs and stops blinking. "You really are clueless."

Tree Girl nods. "He's right. You are."

"Huh?" Jonah asks.

My cheeks heat up. We are not clueless! I do not like being called clueless! I have lots of clues. I feel an urge to roar at Tree Girl, like a polar bear.

Tree Girl pulls a pine needle out of her mouth and says, "You're both coming with us."

"No, we're not," I say quickly.

"We have to rescue our dog," Jonah explains. "He's with the Snow Queen, and he's frozen. We're waiting until the Snow Queen goes on one of her trips. She does a lot of traveling."

"The Snow Queen?" the reindeer asks. "She's evil. Your dog is toast. I hope you said good-bye."

My heart stops. "We're going to save him," I say.

"I wouldn't go near the Snow Queen if you paid me," the reindeer says.

"We *have* to go," Jonah says. "He's our dog."

I notice that now all four of the tree people are circling around us like sharks. Well, like sharks dressed as trees.

"I don't think you understand," Tree Girl says. "You're not going anywhere. You're our prisoners."

It dawns on me. The girl. The family. The statues and forks and other odd things in the sled. These are not nice people who saved our lives. Whatever warmth was in my body drains out of me.

"You're the band of robbers!" I gasp.

All four of them give us wicked smiles.

"They are?" Jonah's jaw drops. "You are?" He makes his air-guitar pose, which is not very funny given the circumstances.

Oh! *That's* why they have all these tree costumes! Not to mention the polar bear and penguin costumes. They wear disguises! To help them blend into their surroundings. They must have been robbing something before they saw us in the lake.

"We take things, yes," the one-eyed mother admits. "And now we're taking you. You're the same age as our other prisoner."

*Other* prisoner? Oh. She must mean Gerda! Just as in the original story!

Mother points to Jonah's wrist. "And we also want the watch."

Jonah clamps his hand over it. "But it doesn't work anymore! It got ruined in the water. See?" He shoves his arm at the woman's face. "It says one thirty. It's not one thirty, is it?"

She shrugs. "I suppose not. I guess you can keep your broken watch."

Jonah hides his hand behind his back.

The mother's face tightens. "Now get in the sled. Or else."

Another tree woman threatens us with her fist.

I gulp.

"What do we do?" Jonah whispers to me.

In the original story, the little robber girl eventually lets Gerda escape. Gerda then comes back to the Snow Queen's castle and figures out how to rescue Kai.

Tree Girl must be the little robber girl. So she's going to let Gerda escape, which means we will be able to escape, too. Hmmm. Maybe going back with the band of robbers and meeting up with Gerda isn't the worst idea.

Maybe it's actually a good idea.

"Get in the sled!" the mother snarls. "Second row!"

And we don't seem to have much of a choice, anyway.

"Let's go," I tell Jonah.

I climb inside the second of four rows. Jonah climbs into the space beside me.

The others climb into the other rows.

"Does this have a seat belt?" I ask.

Everyone ignores me.

I try to calm down. Everything will be fine. We'll hitch a ride with Gerda back to the igloo castle, and then we'll save Kai *and* Prince. Presto, we're done. And that way, we don't mess up the story at all! Easy peasy. Smooth sailing.

Or in this case, smooth sledding.

# * chapter seven *

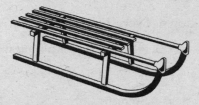

## Welcome to the Basement

about half an hour later, we jerk to a stop.

"Get out," Mother orders.

There is a large house in front of us. It's in shambles. It looks as if it's been abandoned for years. The paint has peeled and it's surrounded by sludgy snow. It is not an igloo castle. It is not even an igloo.

"Is this where you live?" I ask Tree Girl as we all get out of the sled.

"Yeah," she huffs. "Do you have a problem with that?"

"No," I say quickly.

"Put them in the basement with the girl," Mother tells Tree Girl. "And don't forget the reindeer," she adds.

The reindeer, too? He's a prisoner? Why?

We walk into the house, past a crumbling dining room table and broken chairs and half-burned-out chandeliers. In the corner of the room are piles of cutlery, statues, paintings — just like the stuff in the sled. Stuff they stole from other people, I'm sure. They *are* robbers.

Tree Girl leads us to a staircase.

"Here's your new home," she says, giving me a slight push down the stairs. "Don't come out."

Jonah and I head down reluctantly, and the reindeer clomps along behind us.

"Horrid, stupid, miserable place," he mutters.

I glance back in surprise. I'm still not totally used to him talking.

The basement is about the same size as our basement at home. It smells like basement, too. Cold and damp. There's no furniture. Just a pile of brown blankets in the corner. Water leaking from the ceiling has frozen into threatening-looking icicles. There are also patches of frosty green mildew growing on the walls.

At least this basement is bigger than the last location Jonah and I were trapped in, Rapunzel's tower. Although this place is much grungier. And darker. The only light comes from one oval window near the high ceiling.

There's a very skinny girl in the center of the room. She's doing jumping jacks and wearing a bright orange tracksuit.

"I'm back," the reindeer says. "They kidnapped some more prisoners."

"A penguin and a polar bear?" the girl asks between jumps.

"They're costumes," I say, taking off my headpiece. "I'm Abby. And this is my brother, Jonah. Are you Gerda?"

*Please let her be Gerda, please let her be Gerda!*

"Yes," she puffs.

"Hooray!" I exclaim. "It's so nice to meet you!"

Gerda is Asian, with straight black hair that she's wearing in two low pigtails. Her face is heart-shaped and tanner than mine, and she looks to be about my age.

"Oh, sure," the reindeer grumbles in my direction. "Introduce yourself *immediately* to the human. I've only been with you two for hours. Did you introduce yourself to me? No, you did not."

I flush. "Sorry. I didn't realize! It's just that —"

"That I'm a reindeer?" he humphs.

"No, that I wanted to meet her!"

That sounded better in my head.

The reindeer double-humphs and turns up his black nose.

"Don't mind him," Gerda says between jumps. "He's a sweetheart under all the grumpiness."

"Rudolph the grumpy reindeer," Jonah sings, and I laugh.

"You would be grumpy, too," the reindeer huffs, "if the robbers forced you to help them rob people, wouldn't you?"

"I definitely would," I say.

"Also, my name is *not* Rudolph."

"I know your name isn't Rudolph," Jonah says. "It's just a song. It was a joke. What *is* your name?"

He squares his reindeer shoulders. "Ralph," he says.

Jonah giggles. "Close enough."

"Well," I say. "It's very nice to meet both of you, Gerda and Ralph."

"We're sorry the robbers took you prisoner, too," Gerda says, still jumping. "I'm not staying long. I am getting out of here. I have to find Kai. That's why I'm doing jumping jacks. To stay in shape and keep my energy up!"

I clap my hands. "Oh! Kai! We saw him!"

She stops in mid-jump. "You did? You know Kai? Is he okay?"

"He's in a trance," I admit. "He's with the Snow Queen."

"I knew it!" Gerda says, thumping her fist in the air. "I knew he was under her spell."

"He definitely is," Jonah says. "He's not totally frozen, though. He's walking around and building snowmen. He's just kind of spaced-out. He's half-frozen."

"A frozen zombie," I add. "A frombie."

"Ha!" Jonah laughs. "Funny. Not as funny as 'dogsicle,' but still funny."

"The Snow Queen froze our dog," I explain to Ralph and Gerda. "Totally froze. He couldn't even move."

Ralph nods solemnly. "That's what happens when the Snow Queen blows too many kisses at you," he says. "You go completely numb. When she blows you just one kiss, you go just a little bit numb. It's like you're in a trance." He nods at Gerda and says, "Like your friend Kai. But then, with more kisses, your entire body freezes. Even more kisses and you die. That's what

I've heard, anyway. I've never met her myself." A shudder goes through the reindeer's body.

I swallow. At least Prince was alive when we saw him. One more kiss and he might not be. We have to get there FAST.

"I'm sorry she froze your dog," Gerda says. "And I hope she won't hurt Kai." She looks eagerly toward the door. "Sharon said she would let Ralph and me go *tonight*. I told her my whole story and she felt sorry for me. We'll tell her to let you guys come, too! We'll save all of them! Wahoo!"

"Perfect," I say. I like Gerda's enthusiasm. She's what my mom would call a real go-getter. "Is Sharon the tree girl?" I ask.

"The who?" Gerda asks.

"The girl who's dressed as a tree. The robber girl."

"Yes! Sharon is the robber girl."

"Great," I say. This is going to work out perfectly. I grab Jonah's hand and look at his watch. It says it's two o'clock back home. "Do you know what time it is here?"

"Six," Gerda says. "Sharon usually brings dinner down at about eight. Hopefully, she'll let us go then."

I nod. We were right about the time difference. Every hour at home is three hours here. That means we have five home hours left and fifteen hours here. We're cutting it close, but we can make it. This wasn't exactly the pop-in to get Prince that I'd had in mind.

Queasiness settles into my stomach. What if my parents wake up before we get home? For a second, I'm worried I'm going to be sick.

I take a deep breath. I can do it. I can get back to the Snow Queen's palace, defrost Prince, and make it home before wake-up. I can do it! I'm a go-getter, too.

Gerda resumes her jumping jacks. "Come on, guys, let's get some exercise. Who's with me?"

"I am!" Jonah exclaims, and jumps up.

"Why not?" I say, and join in.

"Pass," says Ralph from where he's lying, hooves splayed across the floor.

"One!" Gerda yells. "Two! Three —"

My back starts to feel kind of sweaty. This polar bear costume is hot. It wasn't made to be worn during exercise. Also it's itchy.

I stop jumping and walk over to the corner to sit down. Maybe Gerda can be the go-getter while I *go get* a break.

## chapter eight

## Oops

When Sharon comes back down to the basement a couple of hours later, she is no longer wearing her tree costume. She's wearing black leggings and a long gray sweatshirt. She has blond hair that is stick straight and down to her waist. She's carrying a tray of food and drinks.

"Who's hungry?" she asks.

Gerda jumps off the floor, where she's been resting after her workout. Jonah is sitting beside me. Ralph is napping.

"I'm not hungry," Gerda announces. "I'm just ready to go, go, go! Ralph, wake up! We're going!"

Ralph awakens with a yawn and looks around.

"Go where?" Sharon asks with a sneer.

Gerda keeps her chin up. "You said I could leave. Remember? You felt bad about my friend Kai and said I could go get him tonight."

"Oh yeah," Sharon says lazily. She twists a strand of her blond hair around her finger. "I did say that, didn't I?"

Jonah and I exchange a worried glance.

Gerda puts her hands on her hips. "Yes. You did."

"Maybe. But that was before."

"Before what?" Gerda asks.

I get another bad feeling in my stomach.

Sharon puts the tray of food down on the floor and smiles. "Before I brought friends for you to play with!"

"But they want to come, too," Gerda says, glancing at me and Jonah.

Sharon laughs as though this is the funniest thing she's ever heard. "You think I can let all of you escape? Are you crazy? I can't let all of you go!"

"Why not?" I ask.

"Mother would be furious. I can't disobey her like that. The band would never forgive me."

Jonah makes the air-guitar motion. I give him the evil eye.

"I'm sorry," Sharon goes on, "but with the three of you, Mother can rob all kinds of new places. Like schools! She's making plans. And anyway, Gerda, now you have friends to hang out with down here, so you won't get lonely."

"Hello?" Ralph barks. "Am I invisible? I'm right here! No one was lonely!"

"I don't care about being lonely," Gerda says. "I'm on a mission. I need to save Kai!"

"Why do you care so much about this Kai guy?" Sharon asks. "Is he your boyfriend or something? Do you *looooooove* him? Are you going to *maaaaarry* him?"

"For your information, I'm only twelve," Gerda says, glaring at Sharon. "I'm not getting married anytime soon. But Kai is my best friend and I do love him. And I need to find him." A tear drips down her cheek.

I stand up and put my arm around Gerda's shoulders.

"Jonah and I really need to go, too," I tell Sharon. "We have to get our dog and get back home."

"Yeah!" Jonah exclaims. "According to my watch, it's almost three in the morning at home! We have to move."

Sharon scowls at my brother. "I thought your watch was broken."

Jonah flushes and hides his watch hand behind his back. "Oh! Right. It is. Never mind! What watch? I don't have a watch."

"You're a little liar," Sharon snaps. "And you two should be grateful. You almost drowned. We saved you. Mother is giving you a place to live."

"She's making you lock us in a basement," I say. "And she wants to use us to rob people!"

Sharon shrugs. "We have to earn our keep."

Gerda covers her face with her hands. "Your mother is horrible."

"She's not technically my mother," Sharon admits. "I just call her 'Mother.' All the ladies in the band of robbers do."

Jonah makes another guitar pose. I give him another evil eye.

"What happened to your parents?" Jonah asks Sharon.

"My parents died when I was four," she says, her voice cracking. "They were attacked by wolves."

I gasp. "That's horrible."

Her eyes tear up. "If there'd been a hospital nearby, maybe

my parents could have been saved. But the Republic of Blizzard is short on hospitals. It's a problem."

"So you were left all alone?" I ask her. I suddenly feel really bad for Sharon.

She nods. "Mother found me wandering the woods. She took me in. She gave me food and shelter. She still does."

"And she makes you steal stuff from people," Jonah adds.

"I don't mind," Sharon says with a shrug. "I like meeting new people."

"You're not meeting them," Gerda points out. "You're robbing them. And kidnapping them."

Sharon's expression hardens. "Enjoy your dinner. I'm out of here."

"Wait!" Gerda cries. She presses her hands together and drops to her knees. "Please, please, please let me go. You told me you would let me go."

Sharon shrugs again. "I know I did. But I can't now that Jonah and Abby have shown up. Sorry." She marches up the basement stairs. "Later."

Suddenly, I have an idea. "Come with us!" I call out.

She stops in her tracks but doesn't turn around. "Why would I do that?"

"Because the robbers are horrible people! They force you to steal for them. You said you've always wanted to see where the Snow Queen lives. Now's your chance."

"But where would I live?" Sharon asks, still not looking back at us.

"Anywhere is better than here," Gerda says.

"You're a bunch of snobs," Sharon spits out. "I'll stay where I am, thank you very much." She slams the door.

We hear the click of the lock.

This is not good. Not good at all.

I slump against the side of the wall.

"You know what this means, don't you?" I ask my brother.

Jonah nods.

"What does it mean?" Gerda demands.

I sigh. "It means we messed up *another* fairy tale."

# ✳ chapter nine ✳

## The Great Escape

Let me get this straight," Ralph says, trotting back and forth in the small basement space. His bell rings angrily with every step. "I was finally going to be set free, but now I'm stuck here forever? In this stuffy, dark basement? Because of you two? Is that right?"

"It seems that way," I admit.

"You two are the worst!" Ralph blurts out.

"We're sorry," I say. "We'll figure out a way to escape."

"And what do you mean you messed up *another* fairy tale?" Ralph asks. "Are you in cahoots with fairies? Fairies and witches are a bunch of troublemakers!"

"They really are," Gerda says. She's back to doing jumping jacks. "A witch trapped me in her house for months!"

"This has nothing to do with witches. Or fairies," I say. Even though Maryrose, a fairy, did technically bring us here. What I meant was that since we interrupted the fairy tale, Gerda won't be able to escape and save Kai like she was supposed to. We messed up the story and now we need to fix it. Changing the subject, I turn to Ralph. "How long have you been stuck here?"

"Years," he says. "And I am sick of carting around people dressed as trees and cold-weather animals, helping them steal from other people. It's irritating!"

I hang my head. "It is. And I'm sorry. And I have a plan. I do! We're going to escape!"

"Yeah!" Gerda exclaims, and pumps her fist in the air. "How?"

"I don't know," I admit. "I haven't worked out that part of the plan yet."

"We need disguises," Jonah speaks up. He puts his finger over his lips. "We should wear mustaches!"

"Why mustaches?" I ask.

"They're a great disguise," Jonah explains.

"Oh, sure, disguise yourselves as humans," Ralph whines. "Just forget about me."

I glance down at my polar bear suit and then over at Jonah's penguin suit. "We can't disguise ourselves as humans when we're dressed as animals. But we don't need disguises, anyway. No one will see us! We're going to sneak out in the middle of the night."

"Yeah!" Gerda cheers. "But how? There's only one door."

"And one window," I add, pointing up to the oval-shaped piece of glass. "Is the window locked?"

"Of course it's locked!" Ralph hollers. "Do you think we'd still be here if it wasn't locked? No! We wouldn't! We would have left!"

"Okay, okay, no need to get so mad," I mumble.

"Have you actually checked the window?" Gerda asks him.

Pause.

We all look at the window. It's about ten feet up.

"No," Ralph finally says.

"Is there a ladder in here?" Jonah asks.

"Do you see a ladder?" Ralph barks. "No, there is no ladder! There's no furniture in here at all!"

"Where do you two sleep, anyway?" I ask.

"On the cold floor with the itchy blankets," Gerda says with a sigh.

I study the situation. "Maybe we can climb on each other's shoulders to reach the window and then climb out. Then we'll pull the last one of us up and out with one of the blankets."

"Hello! Hello!" Ralph shrieks. "Is anyone thinking about me? No, no one's thinking about me. You're all just thinking about one another. Do you think I could ever hold a sheet with these things?" He holds up his front hooves. "No. I can't. But it doesn't matter anyway because I would never fit through that window. Never! And you're just going to leave me here! I will never see my herd again! Never! Leave me! See if I care!" He falls to the ground, puts his head on his hooves, and sobs.

Oops. I hadn't thought of that. Ralph is kind of huge. And look at those antlers.

"We're not going to leave you," Gerda coos, petting his back. "Right? We're not going to leave him."

"I was considering leaving him," Jonah admits. "He's kind of annoying."

"We'll come back and get you," I assure Ralph.

"When?" he yells. "Never! That's when!"

"Not never." I think fast. "The rest of us will go through the window, and then one of us will sneak back into the house and unlock the basement door."

Ralph snorts. "Sure you will."

"No, we will. I will. I promise."

"That's risky," Jonah says.

"Well, we can't leave him," I say. I think about FRA. Unlike Robin, *I* would never leave a friend behind. "We're a team!" I add emphatically. "We're FRA! I mean, we're AJRG! Um . . . JARG! Jonah, Abby, Ralph, and Gerda! And JARG doesn't leave a person behind."

"JARG?" Ralph repeats. "What are you talking about? Jonah, does your sister always make up words?"

"Yes," my brother says.

"We are JARG, and we would never ditch our friend!" I cheer.

"Yeah, JARG!" Gerda exclaims. "Go, JARG, go!"

"Will whoever comes back to get Ralph wear a mustache?" Jonah asks.

"Where are you even getting a mustache from, Jonah?" I ask.

"From Ralph's tail?" he offers.

"Whoa, there!" Ralph says, backing toward a corner. "No one is taking any of my tail, thank you very much."

Jonah tries to reach for it. "But it would make a great mustache."

Ralph backs himself into the wall. "No one is touching my tail but me, understand?"

"Why do we need a mustache?" Gerda asks.

*"We don't need a mustache!"* I shout. "Stop with the mustache! Can we focus on the human ladder?"

"Human-reindeer ladder," Ralph growls. "Or have you forgotten about me already?"

"The human-reindeer ladder," Gerda says, patting Ralph on the head. "He's very sensitive," she whispers to me.

"No kidding," I whisper back. "Okay. Let's do this. Heaviest to lightest. Ralph on the bottom. Then me. Then Gerda. Then Jonah. JARG!"

"Go, JARG!" Gerda cheers.

We exchange a smile. I like Gerda. A lot. I wish she went to school with me. We would totally be friends. Maybe even best friends.

I stiffen. Not better best friends than me and Frankie, of course. I would never ditch Frankie. I'm not *that* girl. I'm not Robin.

Jonah eyes the tray of food. "Can we eat before we escape? I'm starving."

"Good idea," Gerda says. "We need our energy. And we want to wait until the robbers are asleep anyway."

"Is there any hot chocolate?" I ask, stepping over to the tray.

"Mmm," Jonah says. "That stuff was tasty. I could definitely have more."

Ralph cackles. "You're kidding, right? They only give you hot chocolate when they're trying to woo you into the sled."

I look down at the pathetic meal. There are four cups filled with gray water. Black flecks float on the surface. There are four limp sandwiches, too. I can't tell what's between the slices of stale-looking bread, but it looks bluish. Gross.

"What about ketchup?" Jonah asks. Jonah is obsessed with ketchup.

I shake my head. "There's no ketchup, Jonah. There isn't much of anything."

"Last time I complained to Mother," Gerda tells me, "she threatened to serve me *reindeer* for dinner."

I almost gag. Ralph lets out a sob.

Gerda nods. "I stopped complaining. So we should just eat what's here." She passes out the sandwiches and cups.

I slowly, nervously nibble on a corner. It's . . . it's . . . it's not that bad. I think the inside is a type of cheese. Blue cheese, maybe?

"It could still use some ketchup," Jonah says. "But it's okay."

We munch away.

"Do you guys know Rorse code?" Ralph asks, his mouth full.

"What's that?" I ask, swallowing.

"It's a way to spell a word by blinking when you can't talk," Ralph explains. "It might be helpful to use during an escape. I taught it to Gerda. We needed an activity in here."

"Wait. Do you mean *Morse* code?" I ask. A long time ago, people used Morse code to send messages to each other.

"Rorse code," Ralph clarifies. "*R*orse. R. Like reindeer."

"Right. Rorse," I say with a laugh.

"Cool. I love codes!" Jonah exclaims, putting down to his sandwich.

Then something occurs to me. "Oh! Is that why you were blinking at me by the lake? Were you trying to tell me something?"

"Um, yes," Ralph says. "I was telling you to R-U-N."

"Oops," I say. "I didn't exactly get that."

"Let me teach you the alphabet," he says. "A is one short blink, one long one, and one short one. B is —"

"I don't think we have time to teach them the whole alphabet," Gerda cuts in.

I nod. "She's right. Maybe we should just make up a code to use if we see Sharon. Or any of the robbers. A code for danger."

Ralph sighs. "Fine. How about two long blinks and one short one? That's S. Like S for Sharon."

"Perfect," I say.

We wait until after midnight to begin our escape.

"Okay. Are we ready?" Gerda asks. She stands up and puts on her matching orange hat, which was under the blankets.

Ralph reluctantly shuffles across the room to stand under the window. "Let's get this over with," he says.

I climb onto his back and then carefully, carefully stand up. I can feel his furry skin squirm under my feet. I hold on to the wall so I won't fall over. "Gerda, you're up."

"Ready!" she sings as she pulls herself onto Ralph's back and stands, lifting her arms into a T for balance.

"Careful!" Ralph whines. "I have a bad back."

Jonah climbs on next. We all hold on to the wall. I try to avoid touching the green mildew.

Gerda bends down, and Jonah climbs onto her shoulders. Then I bend down and Gerda stands on *my* shoulders. The combined weight of Jonah and Gerda is making me tremble a little. I notice that Gerda is wearing purple sneakers. "Nice shoes," I say while I slowly, slowly stand up. "I wish I had shoes instead of polar bear booties."

"They're comfortable, but the shoes I had before were my favorite. They were red. I lost them in the river."

I remember something about Gerda's shoes from the original story. Even though she loved them, she offered them to the river, if the river would give Kai back to her. Which is pretty amazing. Gerda is so devoted to her friend. Gerda is a *real* best friend.

Not like someone I know whose name rhymes with *bobbin*.

"Ready?" I ask. "Let's do it!"

We all stand.

"We did it!" I say.

"Go GARJ!" Jonah says.

"JARG," Gerda and I correct at the same time. She smiles down at me.

"I forgot the blanket!" Jonah calls down.

Oops.

"Of course you did," mutters Ralph. "You guys are the worst escape artists ever. You're never going to come get me. GARJ is short for 'GARBAGE.'"

I bend back down. Gerda bends down. Jonah slides off of Gerda, and then Ralph, and he picks up the blanket. Then Jonah gets back on Gerda. Gerda gets back on me.

"Ready? I'm going to stand up again," I say.

"Ready!" they all cheer.

I straighten my legs. Carefully. Slowly. "I'm up!"

"My turn," Gerda says and then straightens her legs. "Done."

I feel her wobble, but I hold tight to her feet. "Stand, Jonah, stand!" I call.

He stands. "I can reach the window!" he calls down.

"Wahoo!" we all cheer.

"What's out there?" I ask. Gerda's sneakers start to grate against my shoulders. I tremble and hold tighter to the wall.

"I can't tell," Jonah says. "It's too dark out. But I think it's just the ground."

"That makes sense since we're in the basement," Gerda says.

"What are you waiting for?" Ralph asks. "I'm not getting any younger. Open the window!"

Jonah coughs. "Um . . ."

"What?"

"It doesn't open," he says. "I think it *is* locked."

"Well, unlock it!" Ralph orders.

"I don't see a lock. Maybe it's just stuck."

"Break it," Gerda orders.

"With what?" Jonah asks.

"Your elbow! Smash it open! A little bruise never hurt anyone!" Ralph stomps an impatient hoof.

"No!" I call out. "You'll cut your elbow! Jonah, do not smash that window with your elbow! I do not approve of that idea! At all! Are you listening to me, Jonah?"

"I'm listening, Abby. But what do you want me to do?"

"Is there a pole or something we can use?"

"Why would there be a pole?"

"I don't know! Something!"

"There are the water cups from dinner," Gerda says. "We can use the cup to smash the window."

"But then all the glass is going to rain down on us," I say. "We'll be covered in glass."

"I have delicate skin!" Ralph yells. "You cannot cover me in glass! I will bleed!"

"I think if I angle the cup correctly, it will go outside," Jonah says. "We'll have to be careful when we climb out, but we should be okay. I'm coming down to get the cup."

He crouches down. Gerda crouches down. I crouch down.

"I'm not sure about this plan," I say nervously.

"It's the only plan we have," Jonah says.

He gets the cup and climbs back up. He goes on Gerda, Gerda goes on me, same old same old.

"Ready?" Gerda says.

I am not happy about this plan. It has *disaster* written all over it. "Everyone close their eyes just in case!" I cry. I brace myself for falling glass. I can't help but think of the broken mirror in the original Snow Queen story. This isn't the same thing, right?

Jonah starts counting. "One! Two! Thr — Oh! Look at that!"

"What?" Gerda, Ralph, and I ask at the same time.

"Maybe this is the lock?" I hear a loud click. "Yes! I thought it was decoration! Hold on." Jonah opens the window and a gush of cold, fresh air blows through the room.

"Ah," Ralph says. "That feels good."

"I'm going through," Jonah says.

"Careful!" I call out again.

He shimmies through the window. "Pass up the blanket!" he calls.

I bend down very carefully, pick the blanket off Ralph's back, and pass it back up. When Jonah gets the blanket, he holds it down to Gerda and heaves her up and out through the window.

"I'm next," I say.

"No kidding," Ralph mutters. Then he looks up at me with moon-sized eyes that squeeze my heart. "You won't forget about me?"

"I won't! I promise! JARG forever!" The blanket comes down and I grab hold. "We'll come get you in five minutes."

Gerda and Jonah yank me up and toward the darkness.

# ✴ chapter ten ✴

## And Back Again

As I crawl through the window, I enjoy the rush of icy air against my cheeks. "We did it!" I whisper, climbing to my feet.

With the full moon and the stars, it's lighter out here than it was in the basement. The snow of the front yard glows. My hair feels cold, and I realize I forgot my polar bear headpiece down in the basement. It's fine. I'll get it when I go back for Ralph.

"Now, how do I get back in?" I ask Gerda.

"Are you really going back in?" Jonah asks.

"Of course I am," I say. "I promised Ralph!"

Gerda eyes the house nervously. "Maybe we should all go in together."

"We'll be too noisy," I say. "Better for me to do it alone. I'll go and you guys hide out here. I'll be right back."

"Let me go," Gerda says.

"Or me," Jonah says.

"No," I say. "I'm the one who promised him. And I'm very good at sneaking into basements. I have a lot of experience."

"So do I," Jonah says.

"You make a lot more noise than I do," I tell him. He's always crashing into things, and he's not so good at using his indoor voice. "I'll go and you hide out here." I take a deep breath and add, "If I don't come back in twenty minutes, go ahead to the igloo castle, rescue Kai and Prince, and then come back for me."

Jonah crosses his arms. "No way. I'm not leaving you!"

"We're staying," Gerda says firmly. "JARG!"

I shake my head. "It can't just be about JARG. We have to be strategic." I try to sound brave, even though I don't want to be separated from Jonah. I need to protect him, after all. Even though I trust Gerda, the idea of leaving my little brother makes me feel queasy.

Gerda and Jonah shake their heads. I sigh, but I'm secretly glad. "Okay. Then wait for me. If I'm not back in twenty minutes, one of you can come in after me. Then we'll all go together. Okay?"

Gerda nods. Jonah checks his Spider-Man watch to see the time.

I give Jonah a quick, tight hug just in case. It takes him a few extra seconds to let go.

"Be back in a sec!" I say, sounding extra chirpy.

Gerda and Jonah wave. "Go, JARG, go!" Gerda whisper-yells.

I make my way back to the house. Now what? I can't go back through the window, obviously, because then I'll be stuck inside.

Do I just go through the front door?

I might as well try, right?

I run very quietly to the front door. I turn the knob.

It doesn't open.

Who knew? Robbers lock their front door.

I don't know how to break a lock. I am just a ten-year-old girl. Not a robber or an escape artist.

I guess I have two options. I can find another window to climb through or look for another door.

A back door? Yes, a back door! We have a back door at our house, and we always forget to lock it.

I sneak around the side of the house. This time I tiptoe. Not that I'm making a ton of noise in my polar bear booties. At least the moon is bright, and I can see where I'm going.

And I can also see that there is in fact a back door. Hurrah!

The problem is that Mother is sitting on the back porch in a rocking chair, drinking something from a large chipped mug. Hot chocolate, probably. Of course SHE gets to drink as much hot chocolate as *she* wants. I bet she even gets marshmallows. Why is she still up?

I hide behind a tree.

I guess I have to just wait it out. Mother's not going to sleep outside. Eventually, she'll finish her drink and go inside. And when she does, that's when I'll make my move.

Yes. That's the plan. She'll probably slurp it down and be done in a minute or two.

She takes another sip. A slow one.

Another one.

Mother is the slowest drinker of all time.

What feels like ten minutes later, Mother finally, finally takes the last sip. She stands up and stretches her arms over her head. Her one good eye seems to glance over to where I am. But then she turns and disappears inside.

*Whew.*

I wait two extra minutes just to be safe and then sneak over to the back door. Did she lock it? That's the million-dollar question.

I turn, turn, turn the handle. I hold my breath.

It turns. The door opens!

Yay!

Wow, I really have to remind Mom and Dad to lock our back door at home, huh? A crazy person could break in.

I slowly open the door. The house is pitch-black. How will I know where the basement is?

I hear a low voice and freeze.

"They're never coming back. I'm going to be stuck here forever. All alone. I'll never see my herd again."

Oh! It's Ralph complaining to himself. I'll just follow his voice and voilà — basement!

I tiptoe over until I am standing in front of the basement door.

"JARG," Ralph is saying. "Hah. JAG took off and left R to rot."

Now all I have to do is unlock the door and go down the stairs. Abby to the rescue!

The door has one of those locks that pops when you turn the handle. I start to twist the handle and it easily turns. Did the lock pop and I not hear it? I crack open the door.

"Hello?" I whisper. I see Ralph resting on his front hooves in the middle of the room. I jog down the stairs and over to him. "Ready?"

He stares at me. Then he makes two long blinks and one short one.

My stomach drops. The code for *Sharon*. For danger.

"Well, look who came back, after all," a girl's voice says.

I spin around. Sure enough, Sharon is standing in the corner of the room, her eyes narrowed at me.

# ✳ chapter eleven ✳

## Caught

I jump.

Sharon cuts between me and the stairs, blocking my way out.

"Imagine my surprise when I came downstairs and discovered that three of you were gone!" she snarls.

Something silver glints in her hand. Is it a ring? A bracelet? No.

It's a knife. Sharon is holding a knife.

Oh my goodness! Sharon is holding a knife! It's a butter

knife, but still. It's scary! What kind of kid walks around with a knife? A horrible one, that's the kind.

I take a step back and put my arm around Ralph's midsection.

Ralph's eyes are teary. "You came back! You really did!"

"Of course I did," I say. "JARG!"

Ralph sighs. "But I guess now we're not going anywhere."

"Why not?" Sharon asks.

"Um, because you caught us?" Ralph says. "And because you're holding a knife?"

She looks down at the knife in surprise. "This? I was just going to make myself a bagel with cream cheese. I like a middle-of-the-night snack. I can't sleep. It's too hot in my room."

Hope balloons in my chest. "So you're not going to stop us?"

She cracks her knuckles. "No. I'm going to join you! I was just coming downstairs to tell you. I thought about what you said, and you're right. This place is awful. I want out. Anywhere has to be better than here."

"Really?" I ask.

"Really!" she says. "Let's go! I packed us a bag!"

I notice a black duffel bag at her feet.

"After you," I say. But then I push ahead and hurry up the stairs before she does. "Actually, I'll go first." *Just in case.*

"Jonah? Gerda?" I whisper-yell when we get outside.

I don't see them.

"Gerda? Jonah?" I whisper-yell a little louder.

Ralph takes a big gulp of air and extends his front hooves. "It is so good to be out of that basement! Reindeer need to stretch our bodies and our brains, you know. We have extremely high IQs. Higher than humans. Did you know we're geniuses?"

I run farther down the road. *Where are they?* My heart starts to thump. Could Mother have caught them? I turn back toward the house. It's dark. If someone had caught them, there would be yelling.

Unless Sharon has been tricking me the whole time? What if this is an ambush?

"Any chance they went to the ice castle without you?" Sharon asks me.

Hmm. "I did tell them that they should go ahead if I didn't come back right away. . . ."

"There you go," Ralph says. "They probably did that. We can pick them up along the way."

"You don't think they went back into the house, do you?" I ask worriedly.

"No," Sharon says. "The only other way in is through the back and that's how we came out. We would have seen them."

"Good point." I hope she's right. And I really hope Jonah and Gerda are just a little up the road. "Oh," I add, my hands going to my icy ears, "I left my polar bear mask in the basement *again*."

"Take these, Abby," Sharon says. She hands me a pair of earmuffs from her duffel. "Oh, and these." She hands me a pair of brown suede boots.

"Thank you!" I say. "What else is inside? More warm clothes?"

"Yeah. And some food. Carrots and apples and bread. And disguises."

"Really?"

"Of course! If I learned anything from my time with the band of robbers —"

I wait for Jonah to make his air-guitar motion and then feel a lump in my throat when I remember he's not here.

"— it's that you always need to carry disguises. Just in case. Face paint. Sunglasses. Fake mustaches."

"Seriously? Fake mustaches?"

The lump gets larger. Jonah would scream with excitement.

"Of course. The best disguises always have mustaches."

I slip my polar bear feet into the boots. They are huge on me. But beggars can't be choosers. Then I put on the earmuffs, which are nice and cozy.

"I guess we could fly," Ralph says.

"Fly?" Sharon and I ask at the same time.

"Yes, fly," he says. "Have I never mentioned that I can fly? Most reindeer can."

"If you can fly, why didn't we fly around instead of you pulling us all on the sled?" Sharon asks.

"Did you think I was going to tell the robber ladies that I could fly? I have a bad back! I couldn't fit you all on me, and I can't fly with that sled. It's too heavy. Speaking of which, I could really use a massage. Not that anyone ever offered me one."

"Poor Ralph," I say, and give his back a little rub. "But why did we have to stand on you in the basement? Why didn't you just fly up to the window? Wouldn't that have been better for your back?"

He shakes his head. "Reindeer can't fly indoors. You guys really don't know anything."

"So does this mean you'll fly us to the ice castle?" Sharon asks.

"I'll fly you," he says. "But are you sure really want to go there? What if the Snow Queen kisses you?"

"Well, hopefully, she won't be there," I say. I don't add, *She's not there in the fairy tale when Gerda goes back for Kai.* That would require too much explaining. "And you don't have to come in. You can just drop us all off."

"All right," he says. "And then I'll go north to find my herd! I haven't seen them in years. When I was eighteen, I took off to explore. I didn't realize how much I missed them until I got stuck with the robbers." He turns to Sharon. "What about you? Where do you need to be?"

"I don't need to be anywhere," she says with a slight look of sadness. "But I'm dying to see the castle."

Ralph bends down. "Come on, then. Don't be shy. I'm not getting any younger."

"Yay!" Sharon bounces right onto his back. Then she grabs his antlers.

"Do not touch the antlers," he snaps.

"But how will I steer you?"

"You won't," he barks. "I am not a sled. I am a living, breathing, reindeer being. I can steer myself. Come on, Abby, get on. You go in front."

Honestly, I am not sure this is a good idea. There are definitely no seat belts. And I am not wearing a helmet. Maybe we should just walk.

No. Time is ticking. I have to find my brother. And Prince. And I have to get home. Soon. If my parents wake up and find us missing, they'll be so upset. *And* they'll ground us for the rest of our lives. "Okay," I say. I climb on in front of Sharon so I can better look for my brother and Gerda.

First, Ralph starts to trot. Then he picks up more and more speed, going faster and faster, the bell around his neck ringing louder and louder. Then I'm tilting backward and —

We're in the air! We are in the air!

Oh my gosh, we are in the air!

I wrap my arms around Ralph's neck for dear life. *Please don't fall off, please don't fall off.*

"I have to breathe, you know," Ralph calls back to me.

"Sorry," I cry, but I don't loosen my grip.

He swoops up and down. The cold wind rushes against my cheeks like an air conditioner on high.

I am feeling a bit carsick. Make that reindeer-sick?

"This view is amazing!" Sharon cries. "Ralph, you're amazing! I can't believe I have lived with you for so long and never knew how amazing you are!"

I feel him puff up with pride underneath me. It's sweet, but it almost makes me lose my grip.

The view *is* amazing. We're above the snowy trees and mountains. The sun is just starting to come up, and the snow below us is covered in shades of orange and red.

"Wasn't it just night?" I ask.

"The sun sets at eleven P.M. and rises at three A.M. in the summer," Ralph says.

"This is summer?" I ask in disbelief.

"Of course!" he says. "Wait until you see how cold it gets in the winter."

No way am I dealing with a Republic of Blizzard winter. Thanks, but no thanks.

I can't believe I longed for snow back in Smithville.

*Whoosh!*

One of my boots flies off. I knew it was too big. Oops.

"I'm sorry I didn't talk to you more, Ralph," says Sharon. "Mother told me I couldn't, but I shouldn't have listened to her. I was so lonely. And I hated robbing people. Why did we need so many statues, anyway?"

While Sharon is feeling guilty about how she treated Ralph, I'm feeling guilty for letting Jonah out of my sight. I'm his big sister! It's my responsibility to watch out for and protect him. Where is he? And where's Gerda?

"I don't see them anywhere," I say, scanning the ground below us. How far could they have gotten? We should have seen them by now.

"I hope they didn't freeze," Sharon says. "Or get eaten by wolves."

"Oh my goodness, the wolves!" I shout. "I forgot about the wolves!"

"Oh, don't worry about the wolves," Ralph says. "They spend summers in the kingdom of Subzero. They find Blizzard summers too warm."

Yet another reason why I don't want to still be here in winter.

"I'll do another loop to look for Jonah and Gerda," Ralph says. We circle back and then back again.

"Maybe they're already at the igloo castle," I say. I don't know how they could have gotten there that fast. Although they're both in pretty good shape, with their rock climbing and jumping jacks.

"I'll fly over the castle," Ralph says.

The big sparkling igloo gets bigger as we get closer.

I strain my neck to see if I can spot my brother. Something is moving on the roof! Is that them? Is that a penguin? No! Wait! It's Jonah! In his penguin costume! And Gerda in her orange tracksuit and matching hat. She's hard to miss.

"Look!" I say, my body heaving in relief. "They're on the roof! They made it!" I exhale. My brother is here! And I will never, ever let him out of my sight again.

"Hooray!" cheers Sharon.

"Jonah!" I call down. "Gerda!"

Gerda lifts her arm in a wave.

Hooray! She seems perfectly normal! Which means the Snow Queen really *isn't* here and didn't blow any kisses to her.

Prince is on the roof, too. I feel another whoosh of relief. He's in the exact same position he was in before, frozen in mid-gallop. They probably haven't been able to defrost him yet.

Kai is also on the roof. He's lying on his back. It looks like he's making another snow angel. I guess they haven't cured him yet, either.

It's okay. I'm here now to help. We'll have to figure out how to defrost everyone, but at least Kai and Prince are still *alive*.

"So where do you want me to drop you guys off?" Ralph asks. "I'm not sure there's enough room for me on the roof. And I weigh a lot. I don't want to break it."

Kai has certainly been busy. There are three more snowmen than there were yesterday.

"Maybe at the front door?" I suggest. I can see the staircase that leads up to the roof from inside the house.

"No problemo," Ralph bellows. "I can't believe I'm going home. I'm really going home! Thank you, Abby, for coming back for me!"

"Happy to help," I say, feeling warm inside.

"I can't wait to see my herd," he says.

"You're lucky you have a family," Sharon says wistfully.

Ralph not so gently lands on a snowbank. "Good luck, girls."

"You too," I say. I put my arms around his midsection to give him a hug.

"Bye," Sharon says. "Sorry for, you know, keeping you prisoner all those years."

Ralph grimaces. "I know it wasn't your decision."

"But still," Sharon says, hanging her head, "I should have helped you escape long ago."

"Yes," Ralph says. "You should have. Good-bye, girls! Good-bye, Jonah! Good-bye, sweet Gerda!" He waves to all of us with one hoof. Then, with a running jump, he takes flight off the mountain. I watch him sail into the sky, and then I turn around to see my brother.

"Jonah!" I call up.

He doesn't look down. Obviously, he doesn't hear me.

"Jonah!" I call again.

He still doesn't look down. He's very busy rolling something. Is he making a snowball?

Gerda is helping him. She is packing the snow on the ground into a big ball.

Are they making a snowman?

She has a completely dazed look on her face. They both do.

"Why are they building snowmen when they should be defrosting Kai and Prince?" Sharon asks. "Did the Snow Queen put a spell on them, too?"

Dread seeps through me. It can't be. My brother and Gerda can't be under the Snow Queen's spell. The Snow Queen isn't supposed to be here.

"But Gerda waved at me," I say. "Frombies don't wave!"

"Did she?" Sharon asks. "I thought she was just taking off her hat. Look — she put it on one of the snowmen."

Sure enough, one of the snowmen is now wearing Gerda's orange hat.

Oh no oh no oh no.

"We have to save Jonah!" I scream.

"Shhhh!" Sharon orders. "If he's under a spell, that means the Snow Queen was just here. She could be in the castle right now."

I nod. "She's not on the roof, though. Maybe she went to sleep or is out jogging or something. Who knows? We need to sneak up to the roof, get everyone, and leave."

"Yes," Sharon says. "And you know what that means." She unzips her duffel bag. "We need disguises."

I motion to my outfit. "Polar bear isn't good enough?"

She rolls her eyes. "She'll *notice* a polar bear. You need to blend into the background, not dress as something that might attack her."

"Good point. What do you have?"

She rummages through the duffel bag and pulls out a fake mustache. "Mustaches. Tape."

"Of course."

"Sunglasses. Scarves."

"Hmm. But we can't dress up as people. She freezes people."

"I wasn't thinking that we'd dress up as people. We already are people."

I don't understand what she's getting at. "Then what will we dress up as?"

Sharon throws her hands in the air. "Isn't it obvious?"

"No! And we don't have time for guessing games! My brother is in a trance, and my pet is a dogsicle! I am not a master of disguises like you! JUST TELL ME!"

"No need to get huffy," she says. "We dress up as snowmen!"

Ah. I look up at the snowmen on the roof. That is not a bad plan.

"But how do we make ourselves white? Do we cover up in snow?"

"Of course not! We don't want frostbite."

"Then do you have snowmen masks?" I would not be surprised if she did.

"Nooooo," she says, rummaging through her bag. "But I do have white face paint."

We sneak back behind a pine tree and cover our faces with white paint. My polar bear suit is already white, so I'm in good shape. Sharon brought along a white sheet —"in case I needed to be a ghost," she explains — so she drapes herself in it.

"What do we do about our noses?" she asks. "They look like human noses."

"Hmm," I mutter. "Oh! I know! Didn't you pack carrots? To eat?"

"I did!" she exclaims. She reaches into the bag and pulls out a bag of carrots. "Perfect. We'll wear our snacks."

"How are we going to attach them to our faces? I don't think the tape will hold them up."

Sharon sticks one up her nose. "Like this?"

"Ew!" I yell, but I can't help laughing.

She snorts, and the carrot falls out. "Maybe not."

"I hope you're not going to eat that now," I say.

She looks at it with longing. "I'm actually pretty hungry. I never got my bagel and cream cheese."

"What if we just put the carrots in our mouths?" I ask. "Not the gross one, but one of the others. There are so many snowmen, the Snow Queen won't look at us that closely. I'll even tape a mustache to my chin!"

"Perfect."

We grab some branches to use as fake hands, and finally, we're ready. We step out from behind the pine tree and march toward the igloo castle.

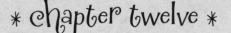

## Snowgirls

t's beautiful," Sharon whispers as we step through the arched
entranceway. "It's the most beautiful place I've ever seen."

Once inside, it *is* kind of nice. If you like white. Because there
is a lot of white. I would not want to drink anything around here
that stains. Like grape or cranberry juice. Although, if it's all
made of snow and ice, it's probably not that hard to clean. You
just scrape.

The main floor seems huge. There are tons of ice corridors
leading off in the distance. Off to the side, I see a dining room

with an ice table and ice chairs. Off to the other side, I see an ice couch. That does not look very comfortable.

The floor is hard and I feel like I'm stepping on packed snow. It's a little slippery, though. It doesn't help that I'm wearing one boot.

Ice columns are everywhere. There's even an ice mantel. On top of it is some sort of broken mirror. Actually, it looks like a mirror that was broken and then glued back together to make a mosaic. It's about twice my size. I wonder if that has something to do with the creepy troll mirror from the original story?

"I'd sleep amazingly here," Sharon says. "It's so cold."

"I would not sleep well at all," I admit. There are not enough fuzzy socks in the world to keep my toes warm.

"I wonder what the Snow Queen is like," Sharon says.

"I'm really hoping you're not going to meet her now," I say.

We creep a few feet more into the house. A snow staircase is up ahead. That must be what leads to the roof.

"So what's our plan to defrost them?" Sharon asks.

"I read, um, somewhere that crying is the key. It melts the ice."

"Us crying or them crying?"

"Both." In the original story, Gerda shows up, hugs Kai, and starts to cry. Her tears seep onto Kai, melting the block of ice in his heart. Then he starts to cry and melts the rest.

"Do you have any onions in your duffel?" I ask Sharon.

"Yuck. Who eats plain onions? That's disgusting."

"They're not that bad," I say, remembering that I had to eat them during my last fairy-tale trip.

Sharon skids on the ice and then steadies herself. "I guess I can always pinch you to make you cry."

Maybe that will be our last resort.

Quietly and carefully, very carefully, we begin to climb the icy staircase. At the top, we see a hatch that's already opened. I step out onto the roof.

Gerda, Jonah, and Kai are all building snowmen beside a frozen Prince.

"Jonah!" I call in a loud whisper.

He looks up at the sound of his name, stares at me for a split second, and then looks away.

"He doesn't recognize you," Sharon says.

"I *am* dressed as a snowman," I say. I take a step closer to him. "Jonah! Jonah, it's me! Abby!"

The truth is that even though I knew he was in a trance, I didn't really think he wouldn't recognize me. How could he not?

Jonah looks back up at me. Our eyes connect. Instead of the usual black pupil in the middle of his familiar eyes, Jonah's eyes are totally white in the middle. He's a frombie.

Not such a funny word now.

He's staring at me as if he doesn't even know me. Me! His big sister!

"You look pretty sad," Sharon says. "Are you going to cry? You have to cry! You can melt him if you cry!"

I definitely feel some prickles in my eyes, but it is hard to make myself cry.

"Come on!" Sharon yells. "Do it. Do it!"

"I can't!"

She pinches my arm.

"Ow!"

"Did it work?"

"No! Let's just get them out of here, and then we'll worry about the defrosting later. We don't even know where the Snow Queen is."

"Okay. Come on, guys, let's go. Follow me," Sharon says.

Gerda, Kai, and Jonah stare at her. They stare but do not follow. They continue building their snowmen.

"They're not coming," Sharon whines.

"I see that! Maybe let's lead them out?"

I walk over and take my brother's hand. It's cold. "Hi, sweetie," I say. "We have to go now."

He blinks his frombie eyes. "Ketchup," he says.

"Ketchup?" I repeat.

"Ketchup," he repeats.

"You want ketchup?"

"Ketchup. Cheetos."

"I'll get you ketchup and Cheetos as soon as we get home, okay? First we need to un-frombie you."

"Flowers," Kai says. "Games."

"Red shoes," Gerda says. "Exercise."

"They are being so weird," Sharon says.

"I think they're saying things that make them happy," I say, and try to yank my brother's arm. "Jonah, you come first, okay?"

"Ketchup! Cheetos!"

"Yes! Ketchup! Cheetos! Come inside and you'll get ketchup and Cheetos!"

"Hello, little friends!" the Snow Queen says, stepping up onto the roof. Her fur cape blows in the wind.

Oh, no!

"Freeze," whispers Sharon.

*Do not move*, I tell myself. *Do. Not. MOOOOOOVE.*

I didn't even have a chance to put my carrot in my mouth.

Sharon did. But she put it up her nose. She really, really did.

And it's staying. She is much better at disguises than I am.

Not only do I not have the carrot in my mouth, but the mustache taped to my chin is getting a little itchy.

No. Do not think of the chin. Forget I have a chin. What chin? I have no chin.

I have a chin! And it's itchy! I will not use the sticks I am holding as my pretend snowman arms to scratch my chin. Even though I really want to.

I will not.

AHHHHHHHH!

The Snow Queen glides by. She doesn't give either Sharon or

124

me a second glance. She buys our disguises. I can't believe it. Not only am I an excellent escape artist after all, but I am also a first-class snowman spy.

The Snow Queen opens her arms toward Jonah, Gerda, and Kai. I expect her to say something mean, but all she says is "Hello again, beautiful friends! Who wants to play?"

Why does she sound friendly?

All three of them smile at her.

Huh? She wants to play with them? Why has she put a spell on them? Why would you cast a spell on someone you want to play with?

And why is my mustache so very, very itchy?!

The Snow Queen holds up a bouquet of red and white flowers. "I don't have ketchup or red shoes, but who wants a flower? I grow hellebores in the atrium! They bloom beautifully in the snow. Kai, I know you love flowers!"

Seriously? Hellebores? Jonah was right?

I'm sad he's not aware enough to rub my face in it.

"Oh, no," Sharon whispers. "I'm allergic to flowers. Ah . . . ah . . . ahhhh —"

"Hold it in!" I whisper back.

"— CHOOOOOO!" An epic sneeze echoes over the roof and through the mountains. The carrot shoots out of Sharon's nose and hits the Snow Queen on the back of her leg.

The Snow Queen whips her head around.

"Uh-oh," Sharon says, and then adds, "RUN!"

# ✳ chapter thirteen ✳

## Choices

I drop my branches and run. Slide-run is more like it. It is harder to run on snow than you'd think. I wish I was wearing Jonah's soccer cleats.

"Wait, girls!" the Snow Queen calls after us. "You can join the others as my special friends!"

"Jonah, come!" I yell as I run, but he doesn't follow me.

I race down the stairs behind Sharon.

Sharon gets to the main floor and heads straight out of the igloo castle.

But I can't leave without Jonah. Maybe I should try and figure out another way to the roof, grab him and Prince, and start knocking on things to find the portal home. I could wait to try fixing my brother and Prince back in Smithville. But how do I get back on the roof when I'm being chased off it?

And anyway, what about the others? I can't leave Kai and Gerda in a trance.

"Where do you think you two are going? Huh, big sister and little robber girl?" the Snow Queen calls out from the top of the stairs.

Jonah, Kai, and Gerda are standing behind her like a frombie army.

Sharon turns around. "You know who I am?"

I duck behind an ice column, hidden from the Snow Queen's view. I can still see Jonah, though.

"Of course I do," the Snow Queen says. "You and your band tried to steal my sled once!"

I make a very small air-guitar pose, for my brother's sake, hoping for a reaction.

There's no reaction. Just more frombie eyes.

"I did?" Sharon asks. "I didn't know it was yours, I swear!" Then she adds, "It was a really nice sled."

"You won't be stealing anything anymore," the Snow Queen whispers before puckering her lips. *"MM-WAH!"* White steam shoots toward Sharon's face.

When it lands on Sharon, the light goes out of her eyes. "Cream cheese," she says in a flat voice. "Cream cheese."

"Now, where did the big sister go? Come out, come out, wherever you are," the Snow Queen says in a singsong voice.

I don't move. I can't let her see me. I can't get caught. I can't! I am the only one left. If she turns me into a frombie, then no one will be able to save us. We will be stuck here forever.

"If you don't come out, I'll just blow your friends more and more kisses," she says. "Then they won't be able to move at all. Like your dog."

I shiver. I also remember what Ralph said. What if she gives us enough kisses to kill us?

"Come out now, and I'll just blow you a little kiss like your brother and your friends. They love it here. I knew they would! I went to pick them up myself at the robber house. They were just

129

standing outside. I blew them a kiss and brought them to their new home."

Oh! So that's what happened. That's why they left. The Snow Queen put a spell on them and forced them into her sled.

"Don't you want to be happy?" she asks. Then I hear, *"Mm-wah! Mm-wah! Mm-wah!"* She's blowing kisses around the room. If they hit someone else by accident, it will make everything so much worse.

She doesn't see me yet. The kisses are ricocheting everywhere, making snow turn to ice and ice to shatter.

I look back up at the mosaic mirror.

Hmm. Is there any chance this mirror is my portal home? Sometimes the portal is a mirror. It doesn't have to be, but it could be. If there is any chance that it is, I could go back through the mirror and get help. I'll get my parents. We'll come back and save everyone.

I step up and knock once on the mirror.

It starts to hiss. It *is* the portal! I knock again immediately and it turns purple.

"Look at you, playing with fire," the Snow Queen says. "That's the mirror that did this to me, you know."

I pause. "It did?"

"A troll tricked me. He knew I was lonely since my mother died, my father was cruel, and I had no siblings. He was standing on the top of an evergreen tree and asked me if I wanted to be the Snow Queen and have everyone be nice to me. I said yes! Of course I said yes. I was only ten! What ten-year-old girl doesn't want to be a queen and have everyone be nice to her? He said, 'Then here's your crown!' And he threw the mirror down on me and laughed as it shattered into glass pieces all over my head. My hair turned silver. After that, I had the power to freeze people. I quickly realized that everyone was scared of me. No one wanted to be nice to me. I had to *make* them be my friends. And the next time I saw that troll, he got what he deserved."

"What happened to him?" I ask, my voice a whisper.

"Let's just say I gave him one too many kisses."

I shiver. "Can you go back to being normal?"

She laughs a sad laugh. "No. I've tried. Besides, I don't want to change back anymore. I'm powerful. Look what I got a nice group of builders to make me! This amazing castle!"

"'Got?'" I ask. "Do you mean you put them under your spell?"

"Exactly," she says. "Usually, I just let the people go after they cook or clean or build for me, but then last year, I thought, *Why not keep one?* I've always wanted a little brother! So I took my sled out and found one — Kai. And then you and your brother came to me. And I thought, why not grab two more? So I took my sled out to get you. I found your brother and Gerda instead. Now look at my wonderful life! I have so many friends!"

"Friends?" I look over at the frombies. "They're not your friends."

Then I glance back at the mirror. What do I do? Do I knock a third time and jump through? Can I really leave my brother? And Gerda and Sharon and Kai?

No. I can't. If they're staying, I'm staying. We'll all be frombies together.

Unless I can somehow convince the Snow Queen to let us go.

"They're not your friends," I repeat. "You're forcing them to hang out with you."

"Who cares?" she asks with a toss of her silvery hair. "I can make people do whatever I want! I *can* force them to stay with me."

"But that's not what friends are," I argue. "Friends *want* to be with you."

The mirror is no longer purple. The portal timed out. Now it's just a mosaic mirror. If I want to turn it into a portal, I have to start all over.

The Snow Queen cocks her head to the side. "It's true that they aren't my equals. I have always wondered what it would be like to have a true equal." She eyes me up and down. "Maybe that could be you."

"Me? Huh?"

"Yes. You. That mirror. It gave me the power. It can give you the power, too."

"What power?"

She stomps her foot against the snowy ground. "The power to have all this! To have whatever you want! To be able to freeze people into being your friend."

So the mosaic mirror has two powers. It's a portal and it gives people freezing magic. That is one extra-special magic mirror.

"My kiss is my only power," the Snow Queen is saying, "but it's an amazing one. Don't you want it?"

I stare at her. I can't help but think about Robin. And Frankie. Was that kind of what I did yesterday? Tried to force people to do what I want? Tried to basically force Robin to be my friend?

"I can see you want to do it," the Snow Queen tells me. "Do it. Smash the mirror on your head! Become like me! We'll be snow queens together!"

Wow.

I did not see this coming.

I wish we could, um, freeze time for a minute so I could think everything through. Of course, part of me is intrigued by the idea of having snow queen power. OF COURSE. How awesome would it be if I could just blow kisses at people and force them to be my friend? Robin would apologize. Frankie would be my friend forever. Even Penny would want to hang out with me — not that I want her to.

But a much bigger part of me thinks that the Snow Queen is totally insane.

Does she really think I'm going to smash a mirror over my head? First of all, that would hurt. A lot. I would most likely get a concussion. And second of all, breaking a mirror is seven years of bad luck.

And I can use all the good luck I can get.

"C'mon," she purrs. "You know you want to."

"I really don't," I say. "I'm not actually great in cold weather. I sleep in two pairs of fuzzy socks. And I'd prefer to make friends the regular way."

"Forget it, then!" she huffs. She pulls her fur cape around her shoulders. "I don't need you, anyway! *MM-WAH!*"

Oh, no.

My head starts to tingle. My eyes burn. I suddenly have the urge to build a snowman and to yell out, "Hot chocolate!" and "Best friends!"

"One more for you," I hear the Snow Queen say, as if through a fog. "I offered you a gift, and you said no. Silly girl! *MMMM-WAAAH!*"

My skin starts to tingle. Everything gets cold. My legs. My hands. My face.

I lift my hands to block it, but it's too late. Now my hands are stuck in front of my face. I can't move them. I can't move anything.

I'm completely, one hundred percent frozen.

# ✳ chapter fourteen ✳

## I Would Like to Move My Hands, Please

I warned you I was going to do that," the Snow Queen says, wagging her index finger. "Tsk-tsk. You are not a very good listener."

I am an icicle. No. An Abby-sicle.

I can't move at all.

Not only do I not have powers, now I am also truly powerless.

The only good news is that I am still alive.

Also, I don't feel cold anymore. But I do feel numb. Like when your leg falls asleep before the pins and needles kick in.

I see my hands. They are both open. They look like my regular hands, only covered with a thin layer of frost. *Move, hands, move!* I push. But they don't budge. It's freaky. It's scary. Poor Prince. He's been like this for over a day!

"You should have joined me," the Snow Queen chides. "There's nothing you can do to save yourself. No one will help you. No one cares about you."

"I care about her," I hear.

Huh? Who said that? Everyone else here is a frombie!

I would turn around to see if I wasn't frozen and all.

*Ding, ding, ding!* Is that Ralph's bell? It is! It's Ralph! He's back!

"Do I know you?" the Snow Queen asks.

*Ding, ding, ding.*

Ralph is standing in front of me now. I can see both of them without moving my head. Which is a good thing, considering I *can't* move my head.

"No," Ralph says. "But I know you. I remember hearing about you, many years ago. I remember how you chose power over friends and family when you were young. I remember how everyone was scared of you and ran away."

"They *did* run away!" she huffs. She turns her back on both of us. "They left me!"

"They were afraid of you."

"And how come you're not?"

"I am," Ralph says. "But I was halfway home to my family when I decided I couldn't leave these kids to fend for themselves. We're JARG."

JARG! My heart melts. The rest of me, unfortunately, does not.

"So you came back to try and save them?" the Snow Queen asks incredulously. "And risk your life?"

"I did." Ralph looks me right in the eye. "I should never have left to begin with. Abby risked her life for me. Gerda risked her life to save Kai. And Jonah and Abby even risked their lives to save their *dog*. A dog! Such a puny animal."

I roll my eyes. They're my only body part I can move.

"No one has ever risked his or her life to save me," the Snow Queen murmurs.

"You have to earn that," Ralph says.

"Earn what?" the Snow Queen asks.

"Loyalty. Friendship. You can't force people into it."

The Snow Queen turns and looks at Ralph. "But how? How could I possibly earn that?"

"Well, you could start by unfreezing everyone."

"Why would I do that?" she asks, her voice chilly. "Then no one would stay here with me! I'd be all alone."

"That's the point," Ralph says. "You have to give them the choice to stay with you. By their own free will."

She shakes her head. "They won't stay. I know it. If I release them, they'll all leave. Would you stay?"

"Me? No. I haven't seen my family in years. I might visit, though."

The Snow Queen is right. I think Kai and Gerda have to get back to their families, and Jonah I need to get home ASAP. But Sharon . . . Sharon loves this place! She thought it was cool, didn't she? Sharon might stay.

Wait. Maybe that's it!

Ralph has to tell the Snow Queen that Sharon might stay! He has to give her hope! And it's not even false hope. Sharon really might. She has nowhere else to go. But I can't move my lips. How do I tell Ralph what to say?

*Oh!*

I wait until I catch Ralph's eye and then I do it: two long blinks and one short.

Then I do it again to make sure he saw.

At first Ralph looks confused. "Danger? Yeah, I know we're in danger. No kidding!"

"Who are you talking to?" the Snow Queen asks him.

I do the Rorse code again.

Ralph's eyes light up.

"Sharon!" he yells. "Sharon will stay! Sharon has nowhere to live! Sharon would stay willingly! At least, I think she would. But we'll never know for sure unless you release her. Unless you release them all." He gives me a wink.

I wink back.

I did it! We did it! Yay, Rorse code!

The Snow Queen looks back and forth between me and Ralph and narrows her eyes. "How do I know you're not lying to get me to do what you want?"

"You don't," Ralph replies. "But you have to trust me. And I think I'm a pretty trustworthy reindeer. I came back to check on my friends, didn't I? I'm risking my life talking to you! Never mind that I'm sliding around all over your slippery floors. You do not want to know what happens to a reindeer with a broken leg. It ain't pretty."

The Snow Queen looks at Ralph, and then back at me again. Then she takes a deep breath.

Uh-oh. Is she gearing up for a huge *MM-WAH* that will knock Ralph off his feet? Is she going to blow me a kiss again?

Is this the end?

But instead of blowing out, the Snow Queen starts sucking in. And in.

I don't know where all the air is going, because she's not blowing up like a balloon, but she keeps inhaling.

A cold breeze goes through me as she does it. I watch Kai and Jonah and Gerda.

Their expressions are changing. Almost as if they're thawing.

Gerda stretches her arms above her head. Kai rubs his eyes. Sharon wrinkles and unwrinkles her nose.

Jonah blinks and then blinks again. He shakes his shoulders as if he's shrugging something off.

"Abby!" Jonah shrieks. He runs over to me and throws his arms around me. "That was so awful! I saw you, but I couldn't talk to you! I couldn't do anything I wanted to do!"

I want to respond, but since I was more frozen than he was, it's taking me longer to defrost. Finally, my arms start to tingle and I can feel them again. Slowly, I wrap them around Jonah. I can't talk yet, but our hug is saying everything our words can't.

"Gerda?" Kai says. "Is that you? You came to get me!"

"Of course I did," she says. She runs to Kai and gives him a tight hug. "You're my best friend."

"I think she loooooooves you," Sharon sings, and then starts to laugh. "I think you looooove each other. You're gonna get maaaaaarried."

"We're only twelve!" they both yell. But they're both blushing.

Who knows? Maybe one day they will.

My lips start to tingle, and I can finally move them. "I am so glad you're okay," I tell Jonah. "I was so worried when I didn't see you outside the robbers' house!"

"The Snow Queen picked us up in her sled. All I really remember is hiding, and then I felt a kiss of cold air, and then I was getting into her sled and we were coming here. And I kept thinking about ketchup and Cheetos."

"All I could think about were bagels and cream cheese," says Sharon, licking her lips. "I love cream cheese. Snow looks a lot like cream cheese, don't you think?"

"Great mustache, by the way," Jonah says.

I rip it off and hand it to him. "It's all yours."

He cheers and sticks it under his nose.

*Ruff! Ruff! Ruff!* I hear from the roof.

Prince is okay! Hurrah!

"Prince!" I yell. "We're down here!"

He comes bounding down the stairs and leaps onto my brother. He licks Jonah's face and then bounces over to me and does the same.

Never has a dog kiss felt so good. Or so warm.

"Who's a good boy?" I ask. "Who is? Prince is!"

"We did it!" Jonah says. Then he looks confused. "How did we do it?"

"Abby and I did it," Ralph says.

The Snow Queen is sitting by herself in the corner. She's extra pale and her eyes are wide and . . . teary? Is it possible? Or maybe she's just cold and exhausted. She did inhale a lot of iciness.

"Are you okay?" I ask her.

"I don't know," she says, her voice shaky. "I've never defrosted so many people at once before. I don't feel so great. But I'm sure you guys want to get out of here. Go ahead. I won't stop you." She sighs.

"We're not going to just leave you after you saved us," Gerda says, hands on her hips. "What kind of people do you think we are?"

"We're JARG," Jonah says.

"No, we're JARGSKSQ," Ralph says. "Is your real name Snow Queen?"

"No," she says. "It's Nicolette."

"JARGSKN!" we all yell.

Prince barks.

"JARGSKNP?" I say. "We could really use some friends whose names start with vowels."


Ten minutes and a few blankets later, we've all completely defrosted. The Snow Queen — Nicolette — has regained some of her color and doesn't look as deflated.

"Thank you," she says. "I feel much better. You guys can go now. I understand."

Relieved, I grab Prince and put an arm around Jonah. Gerda and Kai link arms, and Ralph whinnies happily.

"Go? I have to go?" Sharon asks, frowning. "You're kicking me out?"

Nicolette shrugs. "Don't you want to go home?"

"What home? Can't I stay a little while longer?" she asks hopefully. "I'll be really helpful! I can cook! And steal!"

Nicolette looks confused. "I don't need you to steal. But . . . you can stay as long as you want," Nicolette adds happily, and Sharon smiles. I'm suddenly glad for her — she doesn't have to go back to the robbers.

"See?" Ralph says proudly. "Told you she'd stay." He winks at me again and I laugh.

"How many rooms do you have?" Sharon asks, looking around. "Do you have space for me?"

"There are ten bedrooms," Nicolette explains. "I've always wanted people to come and stay. But no one ever does."

"Oh, I'm staying," Sharon says. "And I bet we could get other

145

people to come, too. We could rent out the rooms! How fun would that be?"

"So much fun!" Nicolette says. They grin at each other. I knew it! The two of them will get along like a house on fire. Well, not actually on fire. You know. It's an expression.

I grin, too. I notice Jonah, Gerda, Kai, and Ralph also look pleased. The Snow Queen really was just lonely all this time.

"You don't play any instruments, do you?" Sharon asks Nicolette.

"No," Nicolette says. "Why?"

"The robbers I lived with were dying to start a guitar band. Every morning, they'd practice, and they were horrible. They gave me the worst headaches."

Jonah's eyes light up. "The band of robbers was really a band?"

Sharon nods. "A wannabe band."

"Ha!" Jonah strikes his guitar pose. "Did you hear that, Abby? The band *was* a band! Amazing!"

I can't help but laugh. I guess I'm not always right. Usually. But not *always*.

I think about Robin, and my cheeks heat up. I guess I was pretty bossy to her. . . .

"Kai and I should go," Gerda says. "My grandmother must be missing us. It's going to take us at least a few days to walk back."

"I can fly you," Ralph says. "It won't take more than a couple hours."

"We have to get home, too," I tell Jonah. "Do you still have your watch?"

"Of course I still have my watch!" Jonah says. He lifts his arm proudly to show me. I'm proud of him, too. Maybe he's not so irresponsible after all.

"It's only five thirty A.M. at our home," he adds. "So we have some time. But I could use a nap before school. And we still have to figure out how to get back."

I look up at the mosaic mirror. "I have an idea."

Nicolette smiles sheepishly. "Sorry that I told you to break it. I'm glad you didn't. It's fun, but not that worth it."

"What's fun?" Sharon asks. "What's not worth it?"

"If you choose to break the mirror over your head, you get snow queen powers," I explain. "Willingly, right? You have to choose to do it?"

Nicolette nods.

Sharon's eyes widen. "Really?"

Nicolette nods again.

Sharon jumps up and down in her spot. "I want to! That would be fun! Would my hair turn silver?"

Nicolette nods. "Yes. But you're better off without the powers. And anyway, you don't want people to be scared of you."

"I love scaring people!"

"She really does," Ralph agrees.

"Sharon, don't take the powers if you can only hurt people with them," I say. Then she'd be just like the Snow Queen.

"But don't you see?" Sharon says, her eyes wide and shining. "There's tons of good stuff I could do with freezing powers. I could freeze wolves before they attack people! And I could help injured people feel better! I could numb their injuries! I could help them think about the things they love. There are *lots* of helpful things I could do."

I feel a wave of warmth. "You are absolutely right."

"She *is* absolutely right," Nicolette says. She hangs her head. "I'm ashamed for not doing all those nice things with my powers."

"Well, we can start together now," Sharon tells Nicolette. Then she heads for the mirror. "Here I go!"

"Wait!" I say. "Do you mind if we use it first? To get home? It turned purple and swirled before, so I'm pretty sure it doubles as a portal. And then you guys can have a mirror-breaking party."

Sharon pouts. "Fine."

Jonah and I start to say our good-byes to everyone.

"We didn't really get a chance to talk," I say to Kai. "But you have a great friend over there."

"I know," he says, putting his arm around Gerda. "She's the best."

"JARGSKNP forever!" Gerda says as I hug her next. "I wish you lived in the Republic of Blizzard," she says.

"I wish you lived in Smithville," I say.

"We would be best friends," we say at the same time.

"I thought I was your best friend," Kai says.

"Don't be silly," Gerda tells him. "I can have more than one."

"Of course she can," I say. And suddenly, I feel kind of silly about the whole Robin thing. Because of course people can have more than one best friend. After all, up until recently, Robin and Frankie were my *two* best friends. Maybe it wasn't very fair of me to say that Robin had to choose between us and Penny.

Next I hug Sharon, Ralph, and even Nicolette.

"Don't worry, I won't kiss you," she says, and pats me on the head.

I stand in front of the mirror, holding Prince under one arm. I take Jonah's hand. My brother knocks once, twice, three times.

The mirror starts to swirl, and we step inside.

# ✳ chapter fifteen ✳

## Back to the Warmth

We step onto the basement floor. I let Prince go, and he rolls onto his back.

"We did it!" Jonah says.

"We did." I let out a breath.

"And it's only five thirty in the morning! We have over an hour of sleep left! Let's get some shut-eye."

We're heading up the basement steps when I hear a creak.

And then the basement door opens.

"Jonah? Abby? Get upstairs this minute!" yells my dad.

My stomach plummets.

Crumbs. My dad is up. Which means my mom is up, too. They know we were in the basement. They know we broke our promise.

Jonah squeezes my arm. "Uh-oh," he says.

"Now!" my mom adds.

I slowly climb up the rest of the stairs. I turn back and glare at Prince. "This is your fault," I say.

He hangs his head. He totally knows it.

My parents are both standing in the kitchen, glowering.

"Again?" my dad yells. "You did this again? Why?"

"We were worried sick!" my mom barks.

"I'm sorry," I say.

"Me too," Jonah adds.

Prince whimpers.

"Where were you?" my mom asks, crossing her arms. "Are you wearing Halloween costumes? Why do you have on white face paint, Abby? And one boot? Whose boot is that? Jonah, there's snow all over you. Were you outside? It's not even snowing. . . . Is that a mustache?"

"I . . ."

I am about to lie and say we were playing in the basement.

But no.

I am not lying anymore. I'm just not. I don't care if the fairy in *Snow White* told me not to tell. What do I owe her? Nothing! Why am I listening to her, anyway? She's just a random person — a random fairy — who told me to lie to my parents. You're never supposed to listen to someone who tells you to lie to your parents! Everyone knows that! People who tell you to lie to your parents are always the ones who are up to no good. And anyway, Maryrose never told me to lie. She never said anything about who I should tell and who I shouldn't.

I take a big, snow-queen breath and force myself to say it. "Mom, Dad, we need to tell you the truth."

Jonah's eyes widen.

I nod. We have to tell them. I know we'll probably have to give up going on our adventures, but I don't have a choice.

"Really?" Jonah asks.

"Really." I clear my throat. "We have a magic mirror in our basement."

My dad blinks. "Excuse me?"

I square my shoulders. "We have a magic mirror in our basement. When you knock on it three times, it takes you into a fairy tale."

My mother rolls her eyes. "Come on, guys."

Jonah jumps on his toes. "We're serious! She's not kidding!"

"We didn't know it was magic at first," I say. "Jonah accidentally bumped into it, and Maryrose pulled us right inside."

"Who's Maryrose?" Dad asks, furrowing his brow.

"She's the fairy that lives in the mirror," Jonah explains.

"Right," I add. "And first, we went into the story *Snow White*!"

"And then *Cinderella*. And *The Little Mermaid*!" Jonah jumps on his toes. "I keep waiting to go into *Jack and the Beanstalk*, but so far —"

"Enough!" my mother shouts. "We don't like being lied to."

"We're not lying," I say. I always assumed if we told our parents, they would believe us. I never considered the possibility that they might not.

"We can show you," Jonah pipes up.

"Oh yeah?" my dad asks. "Okay, then. Show us."

"We probably need to wait until midnight, though," I explain.

"Oh, no," my mom says with a laugh. "I'd like to see right now."

They're mocking us. They don't think it's for real. "But you don't understand," I tell them. "It slurps people up."

"Then it will slurp us up," my dad says.

"I don't think they believe us," Jonah says to me.

I shrug. "They're about to."

I lead the way downstairs. Jonah, my dad, my mom, and a guilty-looking Prince all follow.

"Ready?" I ask.

"Go ahead," my mom says.

I knock. Once. Twice. Three times.

*This is it.*

I wait. There is no hissing or purple light. There is no swirling mirror. No Maryrose voice. There is nothing.

My mom clears her throat.

"Yeah, it needs to be midnight," I say.

"And even then, the mirror doesn't always let us in," Jonah adds. "Sometimes we have to try again another day. Like if we're not wearing the right clothes, or if we don't have a bathing suit . . ."

"Sure, kids," my dad says. "Whatever you say. Look, we love that you have big imaginations, but we do not appreciate being lied to. Especially after we told you not to play down here at night. You promised. And you broke that promise. There will need to be serious consequences."

"But it really works!" Jonah cries. "It does! I'll try again!"

I have a sinking feeling in my stomach. If Maryrose wants to keep my parents in the dark, then she will.

"Don't bother, Jonah," I tell him.

He knocks once. Twice.

"Jonah, stop," I say.

He knocks a third time.

*Whoosh!*

We hear a loud hiss and a purple light washes over the room.

It worked! It really did! Thank you, Maryrose, for not hanging us out to dry!

"What is that?" my mom asks, glancing around the room.

The mirror begins to swirl. My heart starts to pound.

"Hello," Maryrose says from within the mirror. "Bonnie and Dave, please look right here. Jonah, Abby, and Prince, please look away."

Oh, wow.

My mom and dad do as they're told.

"You are getting very sleepy," Maryrose tells them as the mirror twists and swirls.

She is going to hypnotize them! I tear my eyes away from the mirror and look down at Prince, who's burying his head in his furry front legs.

"When you wake up, you will not remember any of this," Maryrose says. Her voice sounds like a lullaby. "You will not remember Abby and Jonah being in the basement. You will not remember telling them not to visit the basement in the middle of the night. From now on, you will sleep very, very deeply at night. You will not punish Abby and Jonah."

"Ever?" I ask, still looking away.

"You will not punish Abby and Jonah for anything related to being in the basement at night. You will forget that they woke you up. Now please go back upstairs and get into your bed. When you wake up, all will be forgotten."

My parents are staring at the mirror with glazed expressions on their faces.

"When the mirror turns yellow, you will both go upstairs."

They nod.

The mirror turns yellow.

My parents both turn around and silently go upstairs.

"Oh my goodness," I cry. "That was the wildest thing I've ever seen! They're not going to remember any of this! Can you believe it, Jonah?"

I turn to Jonah and realize that he has an equally glazed expression on his face.

"Jonah?" I ask, panicked. "Jonah, did you not look away?"

Does that mean he was hypnotized, too?

I tug on his arm. I knock on the mirror. "Can you hear me? Maryrose, you hypnotized Jonah by mistake! What do I do?"

But Maryrose is gone. The mirror has returned to its pre-yellow, glassy color.

The basement is silent.

Jonah is following my parents up the stairs, frombie-style.

I head upstairs, too, and turn off the lights.

My parents go into their bedroom. Jonah goes into his, with Prince trailing behind him. Jonah crawls into bed, still in his penguin costume, and closes his eyes.

What just happened?

I mean, I know what just happened, my whole family got hypnotized. But what does this mean for me? What does this mean for the mirror?

I go into my bedroom and close the door behind me. How am I ever going to be able to fall asleep? What do I do?

I glance at the jewelry box to see what happened to the Snow Queen. Before our trip, she'd stood alone in the snow, looking scary. Now, she's standing in front of the igloo castle with her arm around Sharon. Sharon's hair is still stick straight, but now it's silver instead of blond. I guess Sharon broke the mirror and got her powers, just like she wanted.

On the igloo castle is a sign that says, THE SNOW PALACE HOSPITAL.

They opened a hospital! The Republic of Blizzard really needed one. Now they can help people who are sick or injured. My heart swells. I'm so proud of them.

I glance down at the two loose R beads in my jewelry box.

Proud of them, and ashamed of me.

Robin. Did I really make her take off her necklace? Did I really remove my own R bead — and make Frankie take off hers — just because Robin tried to make new friends?

Was I being no better than the Snow Queen?

I untie my necklace and slip the bead back into its proper spot. I take Frankie's R bead and slip it into the front pocket of my knapsack.

Then I sit down at my desk, take out a piece of orange stationery I got for my last birthday, and write,

*Dear Robin,*

*I'm so sorry. I guess I was just jealous about you and Penny. But of course you can be friends with other people. Even best friends. I hope you'll still be mine, too.*

*Please forgive me?*

*FRA forever.*

*Love,*

*Abby*

I fold the paper, place Robin's necklace inside, and put them in a matching envelope. I'll give it to her as soon as I see her at school.

Then, feeling lighter, I put on an extra pair of socks and crawl into bed.

*　　*　　*

"Good morning, Abby!" my mother says, throwing open my door. Sunlight streams in through my blinds. "How did you sleep?"

How did I sleep? HOW DID I SLEEP? Does she really not remember anything?

I hesitate and then ask, "How did *you* sleep?"

"Really well," she says. "I haven't slept that soundly in a long time. I feel terrific. Come have breakfast," Mom adds. "Your father is making pancakes. Jonah is already eating."

Jonah. Oh my goodness, Jonah.

"Jonah!" I yell, jumping out of bed and running down the stairs two at a time.

Jonah is sitting at the kitchen table. "Dad made pancakes!"

"I see that," I say. "Um . . . how are you feeling?"

"Hungry," he says, and shoves a forkful of pancake into his mouth.

"Yes. I can see that. Did you sleep well?"

He looks at me like I'm crazy. "Yeah. Why? Did you do something to my pillow or something?"

"No." I give him a meaningful look. "Did you have any good dreams? Or scary dreams? Or chilly ones?"

"*Chilly* dreams?"

I step closer to him. "Do you not remember anything?" I whisper.

"What are you talking about? You're being really weird." He downs a glass of milk.

He doesn't remember. He really doesn't remember last night. Does he not remember *any* of our trips? "Can I talk to you in private, please?"

"Now? In the middle of breakfast?"

"Yes." I grab him by the wrist and pull him away from the table and into the hallway.

"Do you remember Maryrose?"

He blinks. "Who?"

Who? WHO?! "The fairy in our magic mirror!"

"We have a magic mirror? Cool! Is it the bathroom mirror?"

"No, it's not the bathroom mirror! You really don't know what I'm talking about?"

He shakes his head. "I can pretend, though. Is this a new game?"

I don't believe this. I sigh. "No."

"Can I go finish my breakfast now?" he asks hopefully.

What can I do? I nod and let him go back into the kitchen. I follow him, my head spinning.

"It's a cold day," Mom says, looking at the weather forecast on her phone. "But sorry, kids. Still no snow."

"That's okay," I say, shivering. "I don't really need snow this winter."

"Snow?" Jonah echoes. Slowly, he turns his head to me. "Wait. I think I had a dream about snow! I can't remember what happened, though. Just that there was snow."

"You were probably thinking of our Naperville winters," Dad says with a chuckle.

I feel a huge surge of hope. Maybe Jonah does remember *something* of our time in the Republic of Blizzard. Maybe his memory of the magic mirror will start to come back!

I just need to wait and see.

# acknowledgments

Thank you to . . .

Aimee Friedman, my amazing editor!

Laura Dail, my incredible agent!

Tamar Rydzinski, my terrific foreign agent!

Deb Shapiro and Becky Amsel, my superb publicists!

To the Scholastic team: This time I will try not to cry as I thank you, but I am truly overwhelmed by your awesomeness. Thank you for everything. Aimee Friedman (so great I'll list her twice), Becky Amsel (same!), Abby McAden, David Levithan, Tracy van Straaten, Jennifer Ung, Elizabeth Parisi, Emily Cullings, Elizabeth Krych, Joy Simpkins, Bess Braswell, Whitney Steller, Sue Flynn, Ryan Lemme, Lizette Serrano, Antonio Gonzalez, and Emily Heddleson.

Emily Jenkins, thank you for reading this book and for once again telling me how to make it better. I am honestly not sure how I wrote and published anything before I knew you.

Katie Hartman and Meredith Bloom for their great catches and notes!

Family, friends, writers, and others: Elissa Ambrose (my mom and go-to proofreader), Aviva Mlynowski, Larry Mlynowski, Louisa Weiss, Robert Ambrose, Vickie and John Swidler, the Dalven-Swidlers, the Finkelstein-Mitchells, the Steins, the Wolfes, the Mittlemans, the Bilermans, Courtney Sheinmel, Anne Heltzel, Lauren Myracle, Emily Bender, Tori, Carly, and Carol Adams, Targia Alphonse, Jess Braun, Lauren Kisilevsky, Bonnie Altro, Robin Afrasiabi, Jess Rothenberg, Stephen Barbara, Jen E. Smith, Robin Wasserman, Maureen Johnson, Adele Griffin, Milan Popelka, Leslie Margolis, Maryrose Wood, Tara Altebrando, Sara Zarr, Ally Carter, Jennifer Barnes, Alan Gratz, Penny Fransblow, Avery Carmichael, Maggie Marr, Jeremy Cammy, and Farrin Jacobs. Special shout-out to my cousin and junior editor, Maddie Wolf.

Jess, John, Stella, and Sadie Green — thank you for the extra push!

Thanks to all the bookstores, big and small, for your wonderful support! Can't wait to visit soon.

Whatever After readers: Thank you for reading and sharing my books. You guys are the best!

Lots of love to my husband, Todd, and our daughters, Anabelle and Chloe. What should we call ourselves? TACS? Or CATS? Love you all the time just because you're mine. And because you're awesome.

# Whatever After #7
# BEAUTY QUEEN

This time, the magic mirror sucks Abby and Jonah
into the story of *Beauty and the Beast*. When they
get this enchanting tale all messed up, the siblings
must make things right . . . or things could get pretty
ugly!

There's a large silver knocker in the center of the blue door. I lift it and let it bang.

We wait. No one comes to get us.

"Hello?" I call loudly. "Anyone here?"

There's no answer.

"It looks deserted," Jonah says.

Prince barks three times and then runs around the side of the castle.

"Wait, Prince!" I call.

We follow Prince and pass an open window. I peek inside.

It's a big dining room. The table is set with fancy plates and all kinds of food.

I hear a growl next to me, but it's not Prince. It's Jonah's stomach.

"I'm hungry," he says.

"Me too," I say. The food smells amazing. Like fried onions and garlic and cheese.

Jonah licks his lips again. "Do you think it's for us?"

"Why would it be for us?" I ask. "They're not expecting us."

"I don't know how fairy tale land works." He sticks his nose inside. "Maybe they're serving French fries and ketchup."

"Let's keep looking," I say. We wind our way around another bend and suddenly we're in a garden. A rose garden. Great. Just what I want to be reminded of. Roses. Big, blooming, gorgeous red roses.

Prince dashes across the garden.

"Prince! Careful!" I don't want him digging everything up.

"Flowers!" I hear Jonah say behind me. "Perfect!"

Prince lowers his nose and starts sniffing around. He'd better not touch anything.

"This one smells good," Jonah says. "And this one. And this one. Ouch! I just cut my thumb on a thorn!" He sticks his finger in his mouth and sucks on it.

I hear a booming voice behind me. "Where did you come from?"

I spin around.

Standing in front of the garden is . . .

Well . . .

He's . . .

He's at least seven feet tall and hulking. His hands and face are covered in brown fur. He reminds me of a dog. But a human dog. His face is wrinkly, like a pug. He has big, shiny black eyes.

This — creature — is looming ominously over Prince. Oh! He was talking to Prince! He hasn't seen Jonah or me yet!

I motion for Jonah to kneel down next to me and hide behind a rosebush.

"Wh-what is that?" Jonah whispers, his face pale.

"I don't know," I admit. Is it an animal? No. It talked. Animals don't talk. Well, sometimes they do in fairy tale land.

I notice that the thing is wearing black pants. And a buttoned-up white shirt and a black jacket and a purple bow tie. But no shoes. Just furry feet.

Huh?

It comes to me.

It's not a thing.

It's not an animal.

It's half animal, half man.

It's a beast. It's *the* beast.

We're in the story of *Beauty and the Beast*!

Photo by Heather Waraska

**Sarah Mlynowski** is the author of
the Magic in Manhattan series, *Gimme a Call*, and
a bunch of other books for tweens and teens.
Originally from Montreal, Sarah now lives in the
kingdom of Manhattan with her very own prince
charming and their fairy-tale-loving daughters.
Visit Sarah online at www.sarahm.com.

Each time Abby and Jonah get sucked into their magic mirror, they wind up in a different fairy tale — and find new adventures!

## Read all the
## Whatever After books!

www.scholastic.com/whateverafter